A
QUIET
STRENGTH

JANETTE OKE

A
QUIET
STRENGTH

JO

A QUIET STRENGTH

A Literary Express, Inc. Book
(a subsidiary of Doubleday Direct, Inc.)
Reprinted by special arrangement with:
Bethany House Publishers
A Ministry of Bethany Fellowship International
11400 Hampshire Avenue South
Minneapolis, Minnesota 55438
www.bethanyhouse.com

PRINTING HISTORY
A Bethany House Publication / 1999
The Janette Oke Collection / 1999

If you would be interested in purchasing additional copies of this book,
please write to this address for information:
The Janette Oke Collection
1540 Broadway
New York, NY 10036

ISBN: 1-58165-112-0

DEDICATION

Dedicated
to the memory
of Sister
Jean Catherine Budd,
who completed her earthly journey
on June 7, 1998.
We will not forget her
devotion, encouragement, and love of life.

JANETTE OKE was born in Champion, Alberta, during the depression years, to a Canadian prairie farmer and his wife. She is a graduate of Mountain View Bible College in Didsbury, Alberta, where she met her husband, Edward. They were married in May of 1957, and went on to pastor churches in Indiana as well as Calgary and Edmonton, Canada.

The Okes have three sons and one daughter and are enjoying the addition of grandchildren to the family. Edward and Janette have both been active in their local church, serving in various capacities as Sunday school teachers and board members. They make their home near Calgary, Alberta.

CHAPTER 1

*R*ather than bouncing from her bed the moment her eyes opened, Virginia took time for a long, leisurely stretch. It felt good to know that her day was not as full of responsibilities as many had been lately. It was her day off from her job at the post office.

Last night her mother had assured her that this Saturday held no special tasks that would need immediate attention. There were indeed the daily chores, but today, unlike so many other Saturdays, there would be more than ample time to do them.

Perhaps, she thought with a smile, she might even be able to talk her mother into a nice little visit to the farm to have tea with Grandma Marty. It had been some weeks since they had treated themselves to an afternoon of warm laughter and quiet chatting.

Virginia stirred. If such pleasures were included in the day's plans, she needed to get going.

She rolled over onto her side and was about to step onto the braided rug when she heard quick footsteps down the hall. A tap at her door, and it was opened enough for her mother to poke her head around and announce, "Virginia, you have a caller."

"Jonathan!" Virginia sprang from the bed, her face flushing with anticipation. She had been waiting impatiently for what seemed forever for Jonathan to return from his trip west.

But her mother was shaking her head, her expression serious. "No. Not Jonathan. It's Jenny."

"Jenny?"

Virginia stood absolutely still in the center of the room. She could not believe it. She hadn't heard from her friend for months. Even Jenny's own father did not receive much news from his daughter. "Jenny? Here?"

Belinda nodded. Virginia wondered why her mother looked so sad. During all those growing-up years, she had always been happy to see Jenny at their door.

"What is it?" Virginia asked, her voice faltering. "What's wrong?"

Virginia saw the tears her mother tried to deny with a shake of her head. Belinda did not answer the question, just rummaged in her pocket for something with which to wipe her eyes.

"What is it, Mama?" Virginia persisted, crossing the room to confront her mother. "What's wrong?"

Her mother fought to control her emotions. "I . . . I'm sorry. It's just . . . just . . . she doesn't look much like our Jenny anymore."

"What do you mean?"

"She's awfully thin and . . . so haggard looking. Like she's already lived a lifetime. And she looks so bewildered and . . . and lost."

Virginia was already hurrying to her closet to grab a

skirt and blouse, then to the dresser for clean undergarments. She whirled about, ready to shoo her mother from the room with instructions for Jenny that she would be out just as soon as she dressed. But she stopped in midmotion to push thick brown hair from her face and look searchingly at her mother. Belinda obviously was deeply troubled. She had not seen Jenny for some time. Had not realized what Jenny's choices and style of living were doing to her health. Her well-being. Certainly this was a shock.

Virginia crossed to her mother and placed hands on her shoulders. "It's going to be all right, Mama," she said, trying to bring confidence to her voice. "She's here now. Don't you see what that means? She hasn't forgotten us after all. She has come home, Mama. We can help her now."

Belinda blew her nose and managed a nod.

"We'll put some meat on her bones. We'll—"

"Did her father tell you she was coming?" Belinda interrupted.

Virginia shook her head. "I don't think he knew either. He was in the post office yesterday and never said a word."

"Maybe she hasn't been home."

"You mean, maybe she came straight here?"

"I don't know."

Virginia glanced at the clock. There was no incoming train until later in the morning. How had Jenny arrived at their doorstep so early? Had she driven herself in a motorcar?

"How did she get here?" Virginia asked.

Belinda suddenly looked confused. "Why, I don't know. She was just there on the back porch when I went to put crumbs out for the birds."

"On the porch? You don't think she was there all

night, do you?" Virginia's question ended in a gasp.

Belinda shook her head sorrowfully. "I certainly hope not. It was chilly last night. Oh my. I'd best get back and put some warm coffee into her."

Belinda turned to leave and Virginia reached for her clothes.

"Tell her I'll be right out."

Belinda paused and faced her daughter once again. "She's not alone, Virginia." Her voice was nearly a whisper.

"Her husband?"

"No. She has a small child with her. I think the little one is ill. She looks peaked and thin."

"Her baby?" Virginia whispered back. She had almost forgotten that Jenny had a child.

"Well, she's not a baby anymore, but she is dreadfully tiny and pale . . . and awfully woebegone looking. Her little eyes are . . . are haunting." Belinda looked like she would weep again.

"Tell her I'll be right out," Virginia repeated as she closed her door, then hastened to slip out of her nightie and into her clothing.

————

Virginia had quickly tried to prepare herself for the meeting with Jenny in the family kitchen. But even with her mother's warning, she found it very difficult to hide her shock and concern. The pale, wasted figure sat half-propped on one of the straight-backed kitchen chairs, wordlessly and aimlessly toying with the handle on her cup.

Jenny did manage a wan smile. Virginia forced one in return. The kitchen clock sounded very loud in the otherwise silent kitchen as she fought for control of her voice.

At last she managed to choke out, "Hello, Jenny."

Jenny did not even answer, just nodded her head slightly. Virginia noted that the life seemed to have gone from Jenny's green eyes, just as the vivid red had been lost from her hair.

"I haven't seen you for a long time," Virginia began, crossing to the table as she spoke. She frantically searched her mind for something to say that might bridge the huge gap looming between them. "How are you keeping? Have you. . . ?"

But she stopped short. Anything she could think of sounded so inadequate.

Jenny slowly lifted the cup to her lips and took a long sip, as though sending a silent message: She would talk when—and if—she felt like talking. Virginia's heart sank, but she nodded silently to herself and moved to the cupboard. Without further comment she opened the small door and drew a cup from a hook. Still not speaking she went to the stove and the coffeepot. Her hand felt shaky as she poured herself a cup and watched the fragrant steam waft upward. She was beginning to regain some kind of composure.

"Your mother was called outside," the voice said in a gruff tone. "Woman next door wanted to show her roses or pansies or something. Said she'd be right back."

Virginia nodded at Jenny's first words. It was a start.

"Would you like a slice of raisin bread?" Virginia asked, feeling thankful that her voice sounded much more natural.

"Do you have oatmeal loaf?"

The request caught Virginia by surprise. "Never understood your fondness for the oatmeal loaf," she said with a little smile, shaking her head. "It's mealy and solid and without much taste."

"That's exactly why I like it. It's mealy and solid. And

it does too have taste," Jenny shot back with a bit of the old fire in her voice.

Without knowing exactly why, Virginia found herself chuckling softly as she crossed to the pantry and the bread bin. Perhaps Jenny—the real Jenny—was somewhere inside there after all.

"Do you want jam?" she called from the confines of the small side room.

"The blackberry," Jenny answered.

"I might have to go down to the cellar. I don't think we have any up here."

Jenny did not offer to change her mind. Virginia was not really surprised. Once Jenny had it in her head what she wanted, there was little one could do to alter it.

"Do you want the bread toasted?" Virginia asked, putting the oatmeal loaf on the table.

"Yes. Toasted," Jenny answered as Virginia turned toward the cellar door.

"Why don't you cut the slices while—"

"I'll wait," Jenny said abruptly, and she took another long drink from the coffee cup.

It did not take Virginia long to collect the blackberry jam. Soon her light step was again echoing on the wooden boards of the cellar stairs. *What is happening here?* she asked herself as she climbed. *Jenny is here. But why? And why is she so sickly looking? So frail? Like she has suffered a long illness or been through some terrible ordeal. What is going on in Jenny's life? How can I best help her?*

But now was not the time for questions. Jenny was waiting for toasted oatmeal bread and blackberry jam. Perhaps after she had been fortified with some nourishment, she would feel more like talking. Virginia certainly hoped so. It was going to be very difficult to be patient as she waited for her old friend to be ready to talk.

"How's your father?" Virginia tentatively asked as she

14

sliced the oatmeal bread. Certainly that was an easy topic that wouldn't offend Jenny.

"I dunno," responded Jenny. "You're more up on that than I am."

Virginia stared in surprise. "You haven't seen him yet? When did you get in?"

"Last night's train."

"Last night? Where did you. . . ?" Virginia bit back the rest of the question. "How many slices of toast do you want?" she asked instead, putting two into the toaster.

Jenny did not hesitate. "Make quite a few. We're hungry."

At the word "we," Virginia's head swiveled and her eyes scanned the kitchen. Her mother had spoken of Jenny's child, but she had totally forgotten. The only chair occupied was the one Jenny was in. Virginia noted that it was the same chair Jenny had always selected in her visits to the Simpson household. Virginia let her eyes travel farther around the room and there, tucked off in a corner, looking even more frail and pitiful than her mother, sat a tiny child with one thumb secured in her mouth. As Virginia's eyes met the uncertain eyes of the little one, the youngster seemed to shrink into a tighter unit, her eyelids quickly coming down. Virginia felt her heart stir in quiet response as she watched the little girl obviously attempting to block herself away from the view of this stranger.

Virginia turned back to Jenny. Had both of them been ill? As her mother had said, the child certainly did not look healthy.

Virginia's fingers fumbled as she lifted out the first slices of toast and added two more to the toaster. "I'll . . . I'll scramble up some eggs," she heard herself saying.

"She doesn't like eggs," Jenny answered in a half-hearted way.

"Some porridge?"

"No. No porridge."

"What can I. . . ?"

"The toast. She's used to toast."

"The oatmeal bread?"

"She's never had oatmeal bread, but if I tell her to eat it, she'll eat it."

The words sounded harsh. Hard. They added more questions with no answers to Virginia's troubled thoughts.

There was silence in the kitchen as Virginia moved about setting the table and preparing the simple repast. Occasionally she heard soft sucking as the small thumb in the corner was more vigorously attacked. Jenny did not stir in her chair or speak. Virginia, thankful the toast was ready, placed it on the table along with the butter and jam and a glass of milk for the little one. She refilled Jenny's coffee cup and poured another for herself.

Jenny turned to the chair in the corner. "Come" was all she said.

The child slid from the seat and obediently moved forward, but the uncertainty did not leave her pale eyes. Virginia felt sure that she would have closed them tightly to hide from the world had she been able to find her way without them.

As the girl climbed into the chair indicated by her mother, Virginia bowed her head and began her table blessing. "Dear Lord . . ." But she stumbled over the next words. How should she pray? Other than being thankful for the food set before them, she did not know how to express her thoughts and feelings, even to her Lord. It was a rather scrambled prayer, she felt, as she said, "Amen." *I wish Mother would get back*, she found herself thinking as she passed the toast to Jenny and moved the jam closer. Their neighbor Mrs. Withers often had something new in her garden to show off, but it was taking far too long this morning.

Jenny generously spread the bread slice with butter, then the blackberry jam, broke it, took a bite, and then passed a portion to the child. The little girl took it with no change of expression, but it was not long before the piece was in her mouth. Virginia had never seen food disappear so quickly. Jenny was also eating as though she hadn't had a meal for some time. Without comment, Virginia buttered another slice, put on the jam, broke it, and placed it on the child's plate. She slipped from the table to cut more slices from the oatmeal loaf. She had a feeling that more toast would be needed.

Virginia found the silence to be uncomfortable, but she knew that she should not attempt conversation before Jenny was ready. At length she ventured, "I . . . I don't think I know your little girl's name."

"Mindy," Jenny answered around the bite of toast.

"Mindy."

"Mindy Anne, but we never bother with the Anne."

"It's a pretty name."

Jenny nodded.

"How old is she now?" Virginia carefully pressed on. Surely the child was a safe subject.

"Soon be three."

She's very small for her age, thought Virginia, mentally comparing the little one to the almost-three-year-olds she knew. She wished to ask if the child had been ill, but she dared not. She noticed the little one squirming as though any attention was unnerving. Virginia would try something else.

"So how long are you staying?" she ventured.

Jenny just shrugged her shoulders and reached for another slice of toast.

"We have lots of spare room now," Virginia hurried to

say. "Only Francine and me still at home."

The words seemed to jog something in Jenny's mind. "How is . . . everyone?"

"Doing great. Clara is expecting her third child."

"Third!" Jenny blurted out, followed by one of her off-color words. "Why three? One's more'n enough to drive you up the wall."

Virginia's eyes flashed to little Mindy. Had she heard the words? Did she understand the meaning? But the expression in the somber eyes did not change.

"Clara is thrilled," Virginia quickly said. "She already has two healthy sons. I think she would like a girl this time, but it won't matter if—"

"She can have mine," cut in Jenny with a forced, hollow laugh.

Virginia chose to ignore the statement. "Rodney is doing very well. Has learned to like the city. He and Grace are expecting their first child. Any day now. Mama runs every time the phone rings. Danny is still in university. He is finishing his course in veterinary medicine. You know how Danny always was about animals," Virginia chattered on into the silence. "He thinks he would like to work in some large zoo. Anyway, he will be working with his beloved animals in one way or another. Francine is finishing up her last school year. She's . . . well . . . you'll meet her later. She spent the night with a friend. She's quite a pretty little thing. Too pretty, I sometimes think, but Mama manages to keep her feet on the ground and her head out of too many clouds. Though it is—"

"And you?" Jenny, finally slowing down between bites, broke in.

Virginia stopped. "Me what?"

"How are things going with you? I thought you would have been Mrs. Jamison long ago. Raising a pack of kids of your own."

Virginia felt the heat rise in her cheeks. "No," she said, shaking her head slowly. "There is another Mrs. Jamison Curtis. A wonderful girl. I'm very happy for them both."

"Jamison dumped you?"

Jenny's voice now held the same aggressive candor as the Jenny of old. *Perhaps the old spunk is still there after all*, Virginia was thinking, feeling some relief that it might be so. She nodded. "I lost Jamison," she agreed matter-of-factly, but inwardly she was surprised. It had happened such a long time ago. Even before Jenny's motorcar accident. Hadn't they talked of it? Or had Jenny just forgotten?

"And you just sit there and take it calmly?" Jenny went on.

Virginia nodded; then a slight smile turned up the corners of her mouth. "I didn't take it very calmly—at the time," she admitted.

"So you let him know he was scum?"

"He's not 'scum,'" Virginia defended stoutly. "He was—is—very gentle and caring."

"Huh," replied Jenny with a snort. "A guy throws you over and you call him a gentleman. Boy, Virginia, you still need to grow up."

Virginia did not know whether to argue for Jamison or rejoice that the Jenny of old was indeed back at her table. But no one had ever been able to provoke her quite like Jenny. She straightened her shoulders and said with some heat, "I am as grown-up as I need to be. And Jamison was right. Oh, I admit it took me some time to see it." She took a breath and continued more calmly, "We were not suited to each other. Not after he left and went to university and got all involved with football. He's playing in the major leagues, you know. Doing well. I would have never liked that kind of life. Away from family. Always gone a lot. I—"

"Football? You're joshing me. *Jamison* a football player?"

"He's in his first year. Quarterback."

"I can't believe it." Jenny paused and her eyes took on a bit of shine. At length she shook her head. It was the same old shake, but the curls looked dull and tired in the morning light. "Maybe I should have tried a little harder," she said, looking coy. "But then, you never would let me even close to the boy."

Virginia thought back to their girlhood. There were times when Jenny had been close all right. Too close. Like the time of the toboggan party. It still made Virginia flush with remembered anger.

"I think I could quite enjoy life with a football player," Jenny mused on with a smirk. "It must be exciting."

It was Virginia's turn to shrug. Jenny's words surprised her. What did she mean? She was a married woman. . . .

"So . . . he finally threw aside all that religious stuff," Jenny observed, her eyes probing into Virginia's.

"He did not." Virginia hurried to set that record straight. "He's more committed to his faith than ever. He uses every opportunity that comes his way to talk about his beliefs. In his last letter—"

"Last *letter*? You mean he still writes?"

"Yes. I . . ."

Jenny's vulgar exclamation in response made Virginia's face flush, and she looked quickly at the child. But Mindy seemed not to notice her mother's choice of words.

"What kind of guy is he? Married to one woman and still writing his girlfriend?" Jenny said sarcastically.

"I'm not his girlfriend, Jenny. I'm just his friend. I'm Rachel's friend too. We write to each other—every week. She's a wonderful person."

"She must be daft. I'd kill Hayden if I found out he was still keeping in touch with one of his old flames."

Virginia felt anger burn her cheeks. She wanted to lash out in defense of the friendship she enjoyed with Jamison and Rachel, but she forced herself away from the subject. Jenny would not understand. The young woman slumped in the chair across from her thought on another level entirely. Virginia swallowed hard and stilled her whirling thoughts and anxious tongue. When she did speak, it was in a different tone of voice and on another subject. "How is Hayden? That's his name? Your husband?"

She saw Jenny stiffen and the spark in her eyes fade. One hand reached up and unconsciously touched at a cheekbone. That's when Virginia noticed the discoloration. Apparently Hayden was not a safe topic either.

CHAPTER 2

"Jenny, what's wrong?" Virginia started to reach across the table but then thought better of it.

Jenny self-consciously studied her hands for a second, then shrugged her thin shoulders. "What makes you think something's wrong?"

"Well . . . I . . ." She stopped and started over. "Things just don't seem . . . right somehow. I mean . . . we're pleased to see you and little Mindy. But coming like this . . . at this hour . . . without letting us know . . . It just seems . . ."

"I didn't know you'd expect an announcement," said Jenny rudely, shifting on her chair. "I used to be able to just drop by and feel welcome."

"And you are welcome now," Virginia assured her quickly. "Both Mama and I are happy to have you come. Anytime."

"Then what's the problem?"

Virginia took note of Jenny's stiff shoulders and jutted chin. This time she did reach out a hand and place it on Jenny's arm. "There is no problem. We just want to be able to help you in any way we can. But sometimes friends just don't quite know how that help should come."

"I don't remember asking for help," Jenny said, her voice as stiff as her shoulders.

"Friends shouldn't need to ask," replied Virginia slowly, her eyes on the bruised cheek.

Jenny did not seem to have an immediate answer. She began to twist her coffee cup around in hands that were trembling slightly. Eventually when she spoke, her voice, though still defiant, held a slight tremble. "Look—if you must know—it's no big deal, okay. Hayden and I just had a little tiff—nothing serious. Married folk do that, you know. I just thought it wise to sort of—you know—take a little break. Good for both of us. With a kid around you scarcely have time to think, you know."

At the mention of the small Mindy, Virginia anxiously looked her way again. But the little girl was leaning back in the big kitchen chair, thumb in mouth and eyes closed. *Poor little thing*, Virginia found herself thinking. *What is her world like anyway?* And then Virginia realized that the little girl was not just closing herself off from her surroundings. She had fallen asleep on her chair.

"Oh my!" exclaimed Virginia, rising quickly to her feet. "She'll be falling off that seat."

But as Virginia moved around the table, Jenny responded in the same tired voice, "She won't fall. She's used to just dropping off like that. Does it all the time."

Virginia was shocked. Didn't the child get proper rest?

"I'll lay her in on my bed. Will it wake her when I move her?"

"I doubt it. She sleeps through anything."

As carefully as possible Virginia lifted the little girl,

featherlight, into her arms. Mindy stirred but did not open her eyes. Virginia carried her into the bedroom and slipped off her shoes as she laid her on the bed. Covering her with a light blanket, she looked down into the little face. Even in sleep it looked troubled and anxious.

"Mindy," Virginia whispered. "I don't know anything about you. Does anyone love you? *Really* love you? Do you know you are loved?"

"Virginia," Jenny's voice called from the kitchen. "I'm going out for a cigarette. Don't suppose you want my smoke in the kitchen. Is the porch swing okay?"

Virginia left the room and closed the door softly behind her before answering. She wished to tell Jenny that the habit she had acquired would bring her nothing but trouble, but she closed her lips tightly on those words and said instead, "Fine. Use the swing."

"Okay if I take another cup of coffee with me?"

By the time Virginia answered the second question she was entering the kitchen. "Sure. Help yourself. Anything else? A piece of Mama's lemon pie?"

But Jenny, who had always raved about Belinda's lemon pie, scrunched up her face. "Oh, no. Lemon pie this time of day? I couldn't face that."

"You used to eat lemon pie whenever you could find it. Morning, noon, or night."

"Well, I don't anymore."

Jenny crossed the room to pour her fifth cup of coffee and fumbled in the coat thrown over her chair, pulling out a packet of cigarettes. "You have some matches? I'm out."

Virginia turned to the metal match holder on the kitchen wall. "How many do you need?"

"A handful."

Virginia cringed at the thought of how many cigarettes a handful of matches would light but filled her fist.

"Have an ashtray?"

Virginia was sure Jenny knew even as she asked what the answer would be.

"Anything will do—old can, chipped cup, tin lid—anything," Jenny said carelessly.

Virginia rummaged in the cupboard's odds-and-ends drawer and came up with a small clean sardine tin. "This do?"

Jenny nodded. "Do you want it back?"

"Put it where you can find it when you need it again," Virginia suggested.

Jenny nodded and almost ran from the room.

I wonder how long she's been wanting that cigarette? Virginia mused as she watched her go. Her eyes shifted to the clock on the wall. *Mama's been gone an awfully long time. Mrs. Withers must really have a lot of new flowers*, she concluded. She wished her mother would come home. Perhaps she would be able to get through to Jenny.

Virginia set about clearing the table. The few dishes hardly seemed worth washing, but she got out the dishpan and filled it with warm water. *Might as well clean them up now as later*, she mused, but her thoughts were out on the porch swing with her beloved adversary, Jenny.

She was almost through the task when she heard voices on the back porch. Peering out the window, she saw her mother sitting on the opposite end of the porch swing from Jenny. Virginia watched as the younger woman held her cigarette down beside her for several moments and talked with Belinda, obviously trying to be civil.

"Go ahead. Finish your cigarette—that's what they call them, isn't it? Do you mind if I just chat while you smoke?" Virginia heard her mother say.

Jenny looked surprised, then confused, then grateful. She lifted the cigarette and inhaled deeply before exhaling in a thin plume. "Spring was late this year," Virginia's mother was explaining in neighborly tones. "So Mrs.

Withers' flowers have been slow in coming. She was very worried that some of them might have winter-killed, and so it is added pleasure whenever one of them decides to bloom. She has these giant day lilies just coming out. Gorgeous coloring. She is so pleased. Just has to show them off."

Jenny gave a short nod in between puffs on her cigarette. Virginia turned away from the window and went back to her dishes.

A small tiff. Was that what Jenny called her disagreement with Hayden? *All couples have them*, she had said. But the discolored spot on Jenny's cheek that she had tried to hide with makeup hinted at something else. All couples did not have disagreements like that—Virginia knew that to be a fact. Never in her family background had anything like that ever happened. Surely Jenny was not in such a marriage. But Virginia knew nothing of Hayden. She had not even known the name of the man Jenny had married until she had spoken of him that morning.

Does her father know about this? Virginia's thoughts continued. Certainly he would not want his daughter and granddaughter to be in such a situation. Never. Virginia could not imagine how her own father would respond in this kind of situation. Her father was very protective of his girls.

But Troy would never treat Clara in that fashion. Any more than Rodney would manhandle Grace. It just wouldn't happen. They had been raised to respect women. To protect and care for them rather than subject them to such humiliation and abuse.

The voices on the back porch carried in through the opened window. ". . . so Virginia has been counting the days. Every morning she hopes that this will be the day he will arrive. It's a good thing she works at the post office. I have a feeling she would be over there anyway, just waiting for the day's mail to come in. He's been awfully good about writing, but sometimes the mail gets delayed or stacked up somewhere. Three or four letters arrive all at once."

"What did you say his name was?" Jenny queried.

"Jonathan. Jonathan Lewis."

"She does like her *j*s, doesn't she?"

"Her jays?"

"Yeah. Jamison. Jonathan."

"Oh," Belinda laughed softly. "I hadn't thought of that."

"What's he like, this Jonathan?"

"Virginia hasn't told you?"

"We haven't had much time to talk . . . yet."

"Of course. Well, he's very nice. We all like him. He came to live next door to help care for his grandmother. Mrs. Withers, that's his grandmother. Virginia was so afraid that someone would move into Mr. Adamson's little house who wouldn't care about the flowers. Well, she needn't have worried. Mrs. Withers is just . . ."

A mewing little cry came from the bedroom. "Mindy," murmured Virginia, drying her hands on her apron as she hurried down the hall. *She's awakened in a strange room. Poor little thing must be frightened half to death.*

She dared not burst into the room lest her sudden appearance frighten the child even further. Should she have called Jenny? Cautiously Virginia opened the bedroom door, expecting to see a bewildered child standing in the middle of a strange room. But Mindy was still on the bed where Virginia had left her, her head on the snowy pillow as Virginia had placed it. Her body had shifted slightly, curling into a tighter ball, and the thumb was still firmly entrenched. The eyes were tightly closed. Already Virginia had become used to expecting the child to close her eyes against anything she did not wish to face, so it took her a moment to realize that the little one was still sound asleep.

"She's just having a dream," she whispered to herself.

And then the reality of it hit her. The dream—whatever it was—was not a pleasant one. A nightmare. Did Mindy have nightmares often? What caused them? Why would a little child cry out in such a way in her sleep?

Virginia stood, one hand on the doorknob, one pressed against her breast. *The poor little thing*. Should she waken her and hold her, or let her sleep? After a few moments of wondering, Virginia backed from the room and closed the door softly behind her. But her mind was filled with even more unanswered questions as she made her way back to the kitchen. What was going on in Jenny's life? What could she do to help?

———

"So . . . you've been holding out on me," Jenny accused, mostly good-naturedly yet with a slight sting. It was Virginia's turn to sit with Jenny on the back porch swing while she inhaled deeply from another cigarette. "Tell me about this guy you've fallen for."

Virginia turned to face her. "Jonathan?"

"I guess, Jonathan. Unless you've got more than one."

"You know I haven't."

"Then tell me about him."

Virginia felt a bit annoyed. She would have told Jenny about Jonathan. Loved to talk to anyone—everyone—about him, but the opportunity had been slightly spoiled by her mother telling it her way. Just how much she had told Jenny, Virginia didn't know.

"What have you already heard?" she asked, trying to keep any edge from her voice.

"Not much. Your mother said you have met him—

fallen for him. He's off west somewhere getting the means to support a wife. You're here waiting, he's a great guy, and that's that."

Virginia felt her feelings of being miffed melt away. She even smiled. "That's it," she agreed. "That just about sums it up."

"Now I want to know the juicy stuff," prompted Jenny.

"The juicy stuff? Oh, I don't think you'd find anything very juicy."

"Try me."

Virginia stirred self-consciously. "There isn't . . . I mean . . . really there is not much more to tell. We're not actually even . . . Really, he's not even called on me yet."

"Called? You mean courted? Called. That's such an old-fashioned term. Fellows don't 'call' anymore—they just court."

"Well, Jonathan will call. He has already promised. As soon as he gets—"

Virginia stopped short. In her determination to defend Jonathan she was spilling out what Jenny might refer to as the juicy stuff. She felt her face flush. Jenny was actually smiling. Well, it was more a smirk than a smile.

"So he's an old-fashioned boy, is he? I should have known." The words carried a tone of scorn. Virginia did not know whether to protest or let them pass. Jonathan *was* an old-fashioned boy by Jenny's standards, but Virginia liked him that way.

"So you haven't made wedding plans yet?" Jenny asked frankly.

"No," said Virginia, her cheeks flushing again. "We haven't talked of marriage."

"But you figure you will?"

"Jenny!"

Jenny just grinned. "Maybe he'll dump you too—just like your Jamison."

Virginia caught herself before she answered. She knew the barb was intended to hurt and anger her. Jenny was proving to be even more taunting and cruel than she had been as a defiant youth. Wisely, before she opened her mouth to speak, Virginia remembered that the words were supposed to bring out her worst. Instead of reacting as Jenny no doubt hoped, she managed to say quietly, "Perhaps he will. If so, then he wasn't the one God had planned for me after all."

"You haven't changed," Jenny snorted contemptuously.

"If you mean, I haven't deserted my faith, no. I don't intend to ever give that up. I couldn't live without the Lord."

"You haven't even tried, so how do you know?"

Virginia paused to search her friend's face before answering. "I haven't tried living without air either," she said slowly, "but I know I couldn't do without it. God is as essential to my being—the spiritual me—as the air I breathe is to the physical me."

"You are too much concerned about the 'spiritual you,' Virginia. You know, science has never been able to prove that we have a . . . a soul."

"I don't need science to prove it."

"You're that sure?"

"I'm that sure."

Jenny puffed out a plume of smoke. "Well, I sure don't intend to let something that I can't see, that I don't even know I have, ruin my life."

Look at you, Virginia's heart cried out in silent anguish. *Nothing but skin and bones, needing that noxious weed every few minutes, on the run from an angry husband who gave you a black-and-blue cheek, a child who looks like a little waif—and you talk about God ruining your life*. Virginia could not say the words. Nor could she control the tears that welled up in her eyes. Oh, if only . . . if only she could show Jenny that God was not a taker of prisoners but a source of real freedom. Of *life*.

The door opened and little Mindy stepped out on the porch, still blinking the sleep from her eyes. Without a word she crossed to the swing and wiggled her small body onto the seat beside Jenny. Jenny did not even reach out a hand to assist her. Silently the little girl managed to turn herself around and into an upright position. The thumb went back to her mouth as soon as she had settled herself.

Poor little tyke, Virginia mourned inwardly, and the tears threatened to spill down her cheeks. "I'd better go see if Mama needs a hand with lunch," she murmured, needing to get away to find some composure.

Jenny lit up another cigarette.

———

"I'd better move it if I'm going to make that train."

The words caught Virginia by surprise. Jenny had popped into their lives early that morning and now it seemed that she planned to pop out again in the same way. "I thought you were staying."

"Did I say that?"

"No," Virginia admitted. "But you said you . . . needed a break."

"And I've had my break."

"It certainly wasn't a very long one."

"I didn't need a long one."

"But your father—you haven't even had a chance to see him."

"I doubt it'll ruin his day. We aren't exactly close, Virginia. Or hadn't you noticed?"

Virginia thought back to the time of Jenny's accident when her caring father had spent day after day by the hospital bed. *Not close?* Virginia remembered his tears. The pleading. The earnest entreaties to the medical staff to care for his little girl. If they were not close, Virginia wondered just who was at fault.

But she could not say all of these things to Jenny. She would estrange the woman even more. Instead she said, "You're sure?"

"I'm sure. I've already been gone too long. I shouldn't have just up and left like that. Hayden will be worried sick about me."

"You can call."

"I don't need to call. I'm going home, Virginia."

Virginia bit her lip. She had no right to try to interfere. "Well—I'm glad you came. It was good to see you again. It's been ages."

Jenny nodded.

"Mama will be sorry that she missed saying good-bye. She should be home from Clara's soon and—"

"The train leaves in half an hour. I still need to buy my ticket."

Virginia nodded in reply. Sometimes there was a lineup at the wicket, but not too often. "I'll walk you to the train," she said.

Jenny did not argue.

It was a silent walk to the train station. Virginia thought back to the time when she had accompanied a very talkative, very lively Jenny to the same train, to make the same journey. It now seemed many years ago. Jenny had been leaving for college then and was filled with all sorts of exciting dreams and plans. Her talk had been about her new clothes and the parties she would attend and the fun that she would have. Well, Jenny had had her parties. She had worn her new clothes. She had flunked out of school, but she had married one of her crowd. In the process, she had very nearly lost her life in a terrible accident. Even now her one hand did not quite function properly. Had it been worth it? Apparently Jenny thought so—she was going back to the same life again.

"Will Mindy sleep on the train?" asked Virginia, concerned for the little girl.

"She'd better," was the gruff reply. "I'm in no mood to be pestered."

Pestered? The child had been a silent little ghost all day long. She acted like she didn't dare let her presence be noticed. Virginia could not imagine her pestering anybody.

"She's a good little soul," Virginia dared observe.

Jenny did not respond at first. Then, after a few minutes of silence, she muttered almost too quietly for Virginia to hear, "Tell that to her father."

The words chilled Virginia. As little as the mother concerned herself with the child, was the father just as bad? Worse? Perhaps even. . . ? The mental image of her father striking little Mindy in anger was too horrible for thought. Virginia shivered even though the afternoon was warm and sunny.

Mindy waited patiently and quietly with Virginia while Jenny got in the short line to purchase her ticket. "Leaving so soon?" Virginia heard Mr. Tuttle, the ticket master, ask. Jenny did not bother to offer a reply. But later, when the two of them stood waiting for the train to sweep around the bend, Jenny did make reference to the query.

"Old Turtle," she began, using the name that she had coined for Mr. Tuttle when she had been a teenager in the town, "is as nosy as ever."

"Not nosy. Just interested."

Jenny just huffed and lit another cigarette.

Thankfully the train was on time. Now that Jenny had thoroughly made up her mind that she would be taking it,

Virginia hoped it would not be delayed. There seemed to be nothing left for the two to say to each other. Most of the talking that they had done had always seemed to end up in some kind of confrontation.

"I'm glad you came, Jenny. Please just . . . just come any time. You're always welcome."

Jenny nodded silently, the only indication that she had any feelings whatsoever for her old friend.

The train was chugging its way up beside the platform where they were standing, puffing steam and billowing smoke. Virginia saw small Mindy shut her eyes tightly against the noise and confusion, sucking her thumb more vigorously. *She's as attached to that thumb as her mother is to her cigarette*, Virginia thought ruefully, turning to Jenny. She carried no luggage, another indication that her flight had been hurried and not pre-planned. She wished to give Jenny a warm hug but wasn't sure how it would be received. She had no idea what to say. How to say it. She felt a wall had been solidly erected between them. "Take care," she managed. It sounded so cold, distant.

Jenny tossed down her latest cigarette and squashed it into the wooden platform with her smart leather boot. She nodded. "You too. And if you decide to marry that guy—Jonathan—let me know. Okay?"

"I don't have your address."

Jenny shrugged. "Well, we might be moving before long, so I guess there isn't much use giving it to you now."

She began to move toward the waiting train, and the silent little Mindy fell into step just at her heels.

Virginia moved along with her. "Keep in touch," she called above the noise of the train.

She wasn't sure if Jenny nodded in assent or not.

Perhaps she was just shaking her once-auburn head of hair. A conductor reached down and swung little Mindy up the train steps, and Jenny followed behind. She did not even turn around for one last wave.

CHAPTER 3

It seems so strange that she would just drop in like that and leave again so quickly." At the supper table, Belinda was still puzzling over Jenny's surprise appearance and then disappearance. "I thought she would be staying with us for a few days."

"She had no luggage," observed Virginia.

"Nothing?" put in her father.

"Nothing."

"You mean she took the train all the way from . . . wherever she is . . . and came up here for a day? No luggage? Not even for her little girl?" asked Francine, sounding as mystified by it all as the rest of the family.

"Nothing," said Virginia again.

"Doesn't sound like she planned very well," Francine noted with youthful wisdom.

"I don't think the trip was planned at all," Virginia responded, concern edging her voice.

"You mean she just up and took the train?"

"Didn't she tell you *anything*, Virginia? I had promised Clara to help her with some sewing. But I certainly could have changed those plans if I'd known Jenny would not be with us for at least a few days."

"I don't think it would have made much difference. She didn't feel like talking."

"Well, that's a switch," remarked Drew with a fatherly smile. They all remembered the old Jenny and her non-stop chatter around the family table.

"She didn't say anything?" Belinda probed.

"Well . . ." began Virginia reluctantly, "she did say that she and her husband—Hayden, she called him—had a tiff. A 'tiff,' she called it. But I . . ." Virginia paused, wondering how much she should say. "I noticed that she had a . . . a bruise on her cheek. She had tried to hide it with makeup, but it still showed."

All eyes were fully on Virginia's face. "Oh my!" said Belinda, hand to her mouth. "The poor girl."

"May be only jumping to conclusions," hastily put in Virginia. "She could have bumped a door. Anything. But she did seem a bit self-conscious about it."

"Oh my," said Belinda again. "Poor Jenny. I should have—"

"Mama, there was nothing you could have done. Nothing any of us can do unless she lets us. We'll have to keep praying for her—and for us, that we'll know what . . ." She drifted to a stop.

"Our Jenny has been so hard on herself," Belinda mourned.

Yes, it was true, reflected Virginia. Jenny had been terribly hard on herself over the years. She was so determined to have her own way, and her own way seemed to bring her nothing but sorrow.

Belinda finally said, "Well, we'll keep in touch. . . ."

"I don't have her address. When I asked about it, she said they were about to move. I don't even know her married name."

"Oh my," said Belinda, distress on her face. "How can we possibly help her?"

"I get the feeling she doesn't want help," said Francine rather dismissively. Virginia noted that her once soft-hearted sister was getting a bit too cynical.

"Sometimes people do not realize that they need help until it's too late," Belinda answered sadly. "I certainly hope Jenny doesn't wait too long."

"It's little Mindy that breaks my heart," observed Virginia. "You saw her, Mama. She will soon be three and she looks not more than a year. She's so pale and drawn . . . and silent. I have never seen such a quiet child. She didn't say a word all the time she was here. Not even 'mama.' And she kept that poor little thumb in her mouth the entire time."

"That's why she didn't say anything," spoke up Francine with an impish grin. "She's been taught not to talk with her mouth full."

"Not funny." Virginia gave her sister a disapproving frown, but she heard her father chuckle softly.

"Well, whatever the circumstances, it appears that our Jenny needs help and doesn't have any friends nearby to whom she feels free to turn."

Her mother's remark was frightening to Virginia. Was it already too late for Jenny?

———

Virginia was beginning to wonder if Jonathan had been a figment of her imagination. Either that or he had gone off home and decided not to come back after all. Perhaps Jenny had been right and Virginia had been "dumped" again. But, no. She had his letters. He certainly wrote like he was coming back, was anxious to get back to her. Virginia clung to that thought even as she much-too-slowly ticked the days from her wall calendar.

She was glad her job at the post office helped to fill her time. That and church activities and trips over to Clara's and taking care of those little ones and helping around the yard and house.

Many free hours were spent with Mrs. Withers. Virginia had promised Jonathan that she would watch out for his grandmother, and she took that promise seriously. Besides, she enjoyed the elder woman's company so it was not a burden. And she loved the flowers. She was so glad that they were being cared for as Mr. Adamson would have wanted. She wondered at times if he was leaning over heaven's picket fence, nodding his approval as he watched them weed and fertilize and prune and stake. She smiled as she imagined his heavenly halo. Was it as begrimed as his old garden hat that still hung in the tool shed? No, she wasn't even sure that people wore halos in heaven. And it was doubtful that there was a picket fence, or that Mr. Adamson even concerned himself with his earthbound flowers anymore. Still it was fun to think about him as she carefully bent over his plants.

"Another letter from Jonathan!" Virginia's whisper could barely contain her excitement as she sorted the post-office mail for each recipient. She wondered how she would ever endure waiting to open it until her noon break. She was so anxious for word that he was coming soon. Would this be the letter that would carry the good tidings?

Virginia lifted her eyes to the wall clock. Only twenty

past ten. With a sigh she returned to her work. Such a long time to wait until noon. Suddenly she was glad that the day's train had brought a lot of mail. The busier she was, the faster the time would go.

She was interrupted many times to wait on customers, so eventually she had to hurry to get the mail sorted into the various boxes before the noon whistle sounded. Just as the wail began to fade, Mr. Manson, the postmaster, stuck his head in the door. "Be right there, Virginia. Just got to finish up this little chore for Mrs. Manson."

Virginia reached into her pocket to finger her waiting letter. It was all she could do to smile politely at the post-man and assure him that he could take his time with the task—whatever it was. Mrs. Pilcher, a new woman in town, chose that moment to enter. She had not yet been assigned a box, so Virginia had to sort through the pile of general delivery to look for her mail. There was nothing there, and Mrs. Pilcher turned away in obvious disappointment. "Thought there'd be a letter from home," she mumbled, and Virginia was afraid that tears would spill when she saw the woman's chin trembling.

"I'm sorry," answered Virginia, understanding the woman's distress. "Maybe tomorrow."

"I tell myself that every day," the woman said, her voice low. "Every day."

Yes, thought Virginia, *I tell myself every day too. I know how you feel.* Her hand reached into her pocket again. The letter was still waiting to be read.

At long last—though in reality the clock indicated it was only ten past twelve—Mr. Manson hurried through the door. "I'm sorry about that, Virginia. Time caught me right in the middle of hanging a new mirror. Mrs. Manson doesn't like jobs half done. You just take this extra ten minutes on the other side of your noon hour."

Virginia nodded and hoped she looked pleasant as she

gave Mr. Manson a final nod and headed for the door. She couldn't even wait until she reached her favorite half-hidden park bench but instead stopped under the nearby weeping birch to pull the letter from her pocket. Her eyes scanned it quickly to see if it gave any indication when Jonathan might return. She would read it more carefully later.

Her eyes soon found the paragraph.

> *"One of these days I will be knocking on your door. Soon, I hope. It has taken much longer than I had thought to get things in order here. It seems I have been gone forever, and I am most anxious to get back. I do hope and pray that you haven't changed your mind and invited one of the local fellows to call. If so, he'd better have a hard jaw because I fully intend to punch it for him."*

Virginia smiled at the attempted humor. He was missing her. Just as she had been missing him.

But there still was no date for his return. With slow steps Virginia started off for home. She needed to get her lunch so she could get back to work on time.

———

Belinda was standing at the gate, waving a hand excitedly in the air. "You're an auntie again!" she called down the street when Virginia was in earshot.

"Really!" Virginia squealed back and quickened her step. "When?"

"The call just came," cried Belinda. "She was born this morning. Around ten."

"Wonderful!"

For the moment Virginia forgot her disappointment. Her brother Rodney and his lovely Grace had a baby girl. She was anxious to hear all about her. She arrived at the gate, panting slightly. "Tell me," she urged her mother. "Tell me everything."

Belinda beckoned her in and shut the gate behind them. "Rodney just called—not ten minutes ago. Baby arrived this morning a few minutes past ten. Grace and the baby are doing fine. She weighed seven pounds, ten ounces and is nineteen inches long. He said she has lots of dark hair and dark eyes. Thinks she is going to look like her mother. He says Grace can hardly bear to have her leave the room to go to the nursery."

"That's wonderful," Virginia said again. "Does Father know?"

"He's out of town this morning. I could hardly wait for you to get home so I'd have someone to tell."

"Mr. Manson was hanging a mirror, so I got a late start. What did they name her?"

"Julia. Julia Grace, after her mama."

"We must let Clara know."

"Why don't you hurry your lunch, and we'll walk over and tell her on your way back to work."

It sounded like a good plan to Virginia. In fact, she would have been quite willing to skip her lunch entirely.

"Don't rush too much," Belinda cautioned later as Virginia bent over her soup and sandwich. "You'll end up with indigestion. We have time."

But Virginia could hardly wait to bear the wonderful news to her older sister—Clara would be so excited. And Francine. She took her lunch with her to school so would not be home until midafternoon. Shouldn't they try to find her and let her know immediately?

"Maybe I'll stop by the school on my way home and see if they'll let me talk to Francine," went on Belinda as if reading her mind. "She'll be so excited it's a girl. I think she's even been praying that way. Though she wouldn't admit it. She insists that 'as long as it's healthy' and all that, but she really did want a little niece. Now maybe she will leave poor Clara alone and stop pestering her about 'no more boys.' "

The two women shared a laugh, a bit giddy in their excitement. A little girl. A little girl for Rodney. They wished they were closer so that they could help with the spoiling. It was going to be so very hard to not see the new little one for some time.

The clouds were hanging heavy when Virginia trudged off to work the next morning. "Looks like we are in for a week of rain," she grumbled to herself, hating the thought. Rain showers were one thing; dull, dismal weather quite another. Virginia had never learned to enjoy a world without sunshine.

She stuffed her hands deep within the pockets of her heavy coat, wishing she could be wearing a bright summer wrap in its place. *By the time I come home tonight the world will be a soggy mess*, she complained further. *Well, at least I will be in out of the chill*, she concluded, pitying the unfortunate people who had to work outside in the sloppiness.

The day was just as Virginia had expected. All day long rain slashed at the windowpanes of the post office, and the wind carried it through the door with each customer who entered the building. The entry was soon covered with muddy tracks that would need to be cleaned away at day's end. Virginia knew that task would be hers before she headed for home.

"Awful cold for a late spring rain," called old Mr. Marshall loudly but cheerily as he stomped his feet, splattering more mud on the already gathering pool. "Feels more like a snowy day."

Virginia couldn't decide whether to merely nod her

head or make some reply. Mr. Marshall was hard-of-hearing and usually misunderstood any words spoken to him. He seemed to feel he could compensate for his deafness by his own speaking volume.

"You been out in this, missie?" Mr. Marshall shouted, splashing through the indoor mud to crowd up close to Virginia's wicket.

"I walked to work in it," she answered with a smile.

"Who?" he questioned, leaning close and rimming his ear with a gnarled hand. "Who was that, you say?"

Virginia pointed one finger at herself. "Me," she answered, raising her voice.

"You? Oh, you shouldn't do that. They're dangerous dogs. Didn't even know we had any of the breed around here."

What in the world did he think I said? Virginia asked herself. *What possible connection. . . ?*

But Mr. Marshall was saying, "Had me one once. Got rid of him. The neighbors were all scared silly of him. Wouldn't even come in the yard. Never did bite anyone, but he sure acted like he'd take a good-sized hunk outa yer leg if you didn't watch yer step. You ever had much to do with them? Who did you say owns one?"

Oh my, thought Virginia with a deep sigh. *How am I going to explain?*

But she was saved by the opening of the door as Mrs. Clemson stepped inside and proceeded to shake a drippy umbrella over the muddy floor. Mr. Marshall immediately swept off his hat, one that had weathered many such rainstorms by the appearance of its floppy brim, and grinned at the newcomer. "Morning, ma'am. And it's a grim day to be out. Only the hearty dare face such a day as this."

The woman grinned in return, revealing a gap in her tooth line. She gave her umbrella another good shake, then tiptoed gingerly through the mud of the entry to reach her post-office box. "Had to come on down," she called over her shoulder. "Mr. Clemson is expecting an important letter, and he hisself couldn't come out 'cause of his gout, you know. So I said as how I'd come on down. Not made of sugar, you know. Won't melt in the wet." She giggled in a youthful way. "Some folks shy away from a little wet weather. Me, I was born on the coast of Scotland. Didn't know there was such a thing as dry until I near reached my fifteenth year." She giggled again. "Oh well, little rain shouldn't keep one to home."

She fumbled with the latch on her box. "Yes, sir, an important letter. We heard that Mr. Clemson's old uncle Bernhardt passed on, rest his soul. Mr. Clemson stands to inherit a good deal of the estate. We're waiting for word from the solicitor."

What in the world would Mr. Marshall make of all *that* stream of chatter? Virginia wondered. Mr. Marshall was holding the battered hat and running trembling fingers through what remained of his hair.

"Well, I sure hope so," the old man said when Mrs. Clemson stopped for a breath. "We could all use a bumper crop this year. Do the whole community good. Whose barn did you say wouldn't be able to hold it all?"

Mrs. Clemson turned sympathetic eyes toward Virginia. "He don't hear none too well," she said in a loud whisper, as though the situation needed explaining.

The Clemson post-office box yielded no letter. Not even an advertising leaflet or a call to join some force to rout evil and entrench good was found. Mrs. Clemson could not hide her disappointment.

"My, they are slow, those solicitors. You can tell it's not *their* money they's concerned with. Old Uncle Bernhardt's been gone for 'most a year already—rest his soul—and we still haven't had the notice of the will."

She shook her umbrella as though she had the solicitor

by the scruff of the neck, gave Mr. Marshall a forced smile and curt nod, and left the building.

"Seems a bit upset," Mr. Marshall said, turning toward Virginia. "I would think that good crops would make anyone happy, even if they ain't on a farm themselves. I always said, prosperous farms make a prosperous town. Don't you think so, missie?"

Virginia dared not attempt an explanation. Just nodded her head in agreement.

CHAPTER 4

*T*he rain was still depressingly steady when Virginia picked her way through the mud of the post-office entry and locked the door on the last customer at the end of the day. She went to get a pail and mop from the storage cupboard. "I don't know whether to sweep it or shovel it," she grumbled to herself. By the time she had finished, the hem of her skirt was mud coated from bending over the grimy mess. Eventually the mop and pail of water looked as dirty as the flagstone tiles. She emptied it out the door.

And I suppose there will be more of the same tomorrow, Virginia fumed with a disgusted sound, peering up at the leaden skies and determining that there was no break in sight. *And likely for many more days to come. I wonder how Mrs. Noah ever made it through,* she mused. *All those days of rain, and all those animals. . . . At least they weren't out playing in the rain and mud, tracking up the floors.* She shut and locked the front door again.

Thumping the scrub pail back into the closet, she plopped the mop down beside it. "See you again tomorrow," she muttered as she pushed the door closed. She stood looking down at her rough, reddened hands. They deserved some of her grandma's homemade hand ointment. Well, they'd have to wait until she got home. But if this rain were to continue—on and on—she would do well to bring a small jar in to work with her. She'd need it, scrubbing out the entry each day.

Virginia thrust her arm into the sleeve of her coat. She hated wearing it when it was supposed to be spring, but she knew she would be more than thankful for it by the time she reached home. She tied a scarf over her hair and prepared for the onslaught of wind and rain as she stepped out onto the sidewalk.

It was as miserable as she had feared. She thrust hands deep into her pockets and lowered her head against the storm.

She would have walked right into someone standing beneath the weeping birch had not a hand reached out to touch her shoulder. Startled, Virginia's head came upright as she stopped abruptly. A tall man, bundled in dark clothes against the unspringlike weather, stood solidly in the path in front of her.

"Virginia."

Virginia's breath caught in her throat. Was she dreaming? "Jonathan?"

"I've been waiting. . . ."

Suddenly it did not matter about the rain. About the mud in the entry or the heavy coat. It could rain all it wanted. Nothing—nothing in all the world—mattered, except that he was there. He was finally there. He had come back. He was waiting.

"Oh, Jonathan" was her glad cry, and then she was in

his arms, weeping against the rough wool of the broad-shouldered jacket.

He held her. Just held her and let her weep. She wondered if he was weeping too, but she could not tell for the constant stream of rain that ran over both of them. At length he kissed the top of her wet head. "I need to get you home," he whispered. "You're soaked."

Virginia laughed. Laughed at the rain that had made her so despondent such a short time earlier. "You look a little wet yourself," she informed him.

He laughed with her. "Guess I am. That birch isn't all that great as a shelter."

"How long have you been here?"

"Under this tree, or in town?"

"Both, I guess."

"Well, I came in on this morning's train. Had to get the horses out to the farm and into the corrals. They'd had enough of train travel. Soon as I got them settled I came into town. Couldn't wait for your day to end. . . ." He stopped and looked into her eyes. The cloudy skies and damp surroundings did not make for good lighting, but Virginia saw the love and eagerness in the gaze. *You were wrong, Jenny*, she said in her heart. *He came back.*

"As to how long I've been here under this dripping birch—only an eon or two, I guess. It seems like a very long time." His arms tightened about her. Virginia's reached up to encircle his neck. *Oh dear*, she found herself thinking. *He has not even officially come calling yet, and here we are in an embrace. On Main Street. Just as though . . . as though . . . it was all settled.*

The thought did not make her back away. She looked up into Jonathan's face and smiled. "I think we'd better get out of the rain," she said softly. "I want to hear all about your trip west. We have so much to talk about."

"We do," he agreed. "We surely do."

51

He kissed her dripping hair once more before releasing her, and Virginia stepped back and smiled at him again. There was no use trying to straighten rumpled clothes. The rain had them both a wrinkled, sodden mess. They merely smiled at each other, then started down the street, her arm tucked protectively in his.

"You know, I never cared much for the rain," Jonathan said in a teasing tone, "but I have the feeling that from now on it might hold a charm all its own."

Virginia looked at him, saw the glint in his eyes, and understood. "I hate the rain," she nodded. "I always have."

"Well, look at you. Look at me. If this had been a normal day, if I had walked up to the post-office door and met you as you left—in broad daylight and bright sunshine—would you have welcomed me in the same way?"

Oh, Jonathan, I missed you so much, Virginia's heart cried. *Every day I've longed for you to come back*. But Jonathan was continuing.

"The rain, the storm, the chilliness . . . it . . . Well, I think the gloominess of it all represented our moods while we were apart. So in a way it . . . sort of drew us together, knowing that if we were together again, it wouldn't matter about . . . about other things. Rain. Hail. Snow. Life itself. We need to be together. Even the rain is okay if we're together."

He put his free hand over hers on his arm. Virginia could feel the lump in her throat. Her eyes threatened to add salty tears to the moisture that ran down her cheeks.

"Do you know what I'm trying to say, Virginia?"

She tried to answer, but her throat was so tight words would not come. She nodded her head in agreement. Then Jonathan stopped walking and turned her to face him. He lifted her face with a hand under her trembling chin and looked deeply into her eyes. "Before I left I knew that I loved you, but I had no idea how hard it would be to be away from you. I don't want to be apart again. Not ever." He hesitated for a moment, studying her face. "Do you understand, Virginia?"

Virginia managed a nod in spite of the hand supporting her chin.

"I love you. I want to marry you. And it might be selfish of me, but I don't want to wait. It's been too long already. Will you marry me, Virginia?"

The rain continued to caress Virginia's upturned face. She blinked the moisture from her eyelids, knowing that more warm tears were joining the cold splashes of raindrops. She swallowed hard to get control of her voice and her emotions. How she had longed to hear those words from Jonathan. "Yes," she answered, and her voice was surprisingly strong in spite of her trembling. "Yes."

"Soon?"

"Yes." There was absolutely no doubt in her mind.

And then Jonathan was kissing her. Not on her rain-wet hair but on her lips. And Virginia had one ridiculous thought that almost brought a chuckle: *So much for long months of traditional parlor calling.*

In a small wedding with little fuss or flourish, they were married in just two weeks on a Saturday. Virginia could not help but think back to the glorious event that had launched her brother Rodney's marriage to Grace, even though that wedding was still simple by society's standards. But her own wedding's lack of frills and finery did not dampen Virginia's spirits. And, yes, neither did the rain.

She borrowed Clara's gown, thankful that it did not need alterations. She wore her mother's veil and carried flowers from Mrs. Withers' garden. The church, too, was graced with large bouquets. Virginia was sure Mr. Adamson would have been pleased to see his flowers standing tall and proud in the two milk white vases.

Jonathan told Virginia that he had talked about her with his parents before he left the West. Had explained his intentions to ask her to marry him. They wanted to be at the wedding, but of course the time and distance made that impossible. Damaris Lewis wrote to welcome Virginia to their family and noted that she was glad to have had the opportunity to meet Virginia, even briefly, when settling her mother into the Adamson house.

With no one to care for Jonathan's horses, there would be no wedding trip. But Virginia had assured him that she did not mind. Perhaps one day, after they were established, they could take an anniversary trip instead.

And they would have no home of their own. Virginia had also tried to reassure Jonathan on that account. She loved his grandmother. Enjoyed the woman's company. She would be pleased to share the older woman's home until Jonathan was able to build their own at the farm. It would be no hardship at all. At least they would be together. That was what mattered.

After some discussion, they decided that Virginia would continue her job. The income would assist them greatly in saving for the house Jonathan planned to build. Getting his start as a breeder of fine horses would require both time and energy. It could be years before he began to reap returns for his labor.

But they were pulling together—that was the fact that made the dream not so far away. That was what made Virginia hum to herself as she prepared for work the Monday morning following their marriage.

In the days that had preceded their Saturday wedding, her time had been taken getting the simple plans quickly in place. She would never have made it without the help of her loving and supportive family. She smiled as she remembered the play of emotions on her parents' faces when Jonathan had asked for their daughter's hand in marriage—in just two weeks! But they gamely had pitched in, and now she was Mrs. Jonathan Lewis. Virginia Lewis. She would need to get used to her new name. "Virginia Lewis" sounded wonderful.

Jonathan had left early for the farm. He had much to do, he had said, but couldn't wait to be with her again at day's end. He had held her closely for a long time, as though it was difficult for him to let her go. "I love you, Mrs. Lewis," he had whispered into her hair, and she had thrilled at the words.

"It won't be long," she had promised, smiling. "I'll be here when you get home."

Already her mind was whirling with plans. She would have a special meal ready for her new husband when he came home at the end of the day. She would shop during her lunch hour and then pick up the meat from the butcher as she passed on her way home. Jonathan liked raisin pie. She would just have time to bake one. And biscuits. She would make a pan of fresh, warm biscuits to go with the fried chicken and milk gravy.

Virginia left the small back bedroom that she now shared with Jonathan, still humming to herself. Another rain shower was drenching the world outside the living room window, but even that could not dampen her spirits. She smiled softly to herself, sure that it would be as Jonathan had said: Rain would always have pleasant memories for her now. It was in the rain that Jonathan had first told her that he loved her.

Grandmother Withers was seated at the kitchen table, her Bible spread before her. She smiled when Virginia entered the room.

"My, don't you look like a day in summer," she welcomed her new granddaughter.

"Good morning, Grandmother," Virginia responded.

"Jonathan said you needed a little extra sleep this morning. What with wedding preparations and all, you've had a busy time of it."

Virginia had to agree.

"I gave Jonathan his breakfast and sent him off with a lunch. He said he'd try to be home by six."

Yes, thought Virginia. *Jonathan did not go without speaking with me. I know his plans for the day.*

She leaned over and placed a kiss on the older woman's white hair. "Thank you," she said, the joy of the morning still giving sparkle to her words.

"There is porridge on the back of the stove."

"Oh, I don't need more than a slice of toast."

"Toast? That's not enough to get you through the day. Best you have a little porridge. It's damp and cold out there again. You'll need some nourishment to keep you from the ague. Nothing like porridge to stick to your bones and give you resistance."

Virginia chuckled. It was rather nice to have someone fussing over her.

"Okay, Grandmother. Porridge it will be."

She helped herself to a small serving, feeling hard put not to remind herself of just how much she disliked it. Sometime around her eleventh birthday, her mother had finally relented and not demanded that she eat it anymore. Now it was back to porridge once again.

Well, it wouldn't be for long. Once she and Jonathan were in their own home, she would gladly make morning porridge for him if he liked, but she would not force down a bowl of it herself.

It was all Virginia could do to finish the bowl now. She was thankful when the last spoonful was swallowed. One glance at the clock told her that she must hurry. She crossed to the stove and filled the dishpan with warm water to begin the cleaning up chores.

"This Scripture has always puzzled me," said Mrs. Withers.

Virginia looked around.

"Christ told his disciples that we are to hate our mother and father and follow Him. Why would He say that when we are commanded over and over to love?"

Virginia tried to concentrate on the seeming contradiction, but her mind still kept jumping to her plans for dinner. "I . . . I don't think that He really meant 'hate'."

"But it says hate. Right here."

"I think the meaning is more . . . well . . . putting things, including people, in proper order. We are not to love family—anyone—above Christ himself. It is not family members who are to govern our lives. He is to come first—always."

"But it says hate. Right here," she repeated. Obviously Virginia's explanation hadn't helped.

"Why don't you ask the pastor about it the next time he calls?"

There was silence for a few moments as Mrs. Withers considered the suggestion. "Yes," she said at last. "Yes, I think I'll do that. He'll know, won't he?"

"I'm sure he will."

"Will you be home at noon?"

Virginia thought of her plans for shopping. "No, not today. Most days I will, but not today."

"But you don't have a lunch to take with you. I didn't know you weren't planning to be home or I would have made yours when I made Jonathan's."

"It's fine, Grandmother. I'll grab an apple from the root cellar on my way out."

"But an apple isn't enough."

"It'll be all right. Just this once."

"You should care for your body, you know. A woman has to think ahead. One cannot produce healthy children unless one is healthy."

Virginia had not been thinking of children. She felt her face flush. "I'll cut a piece of cheese as well," she promised.

Mrs. Withers seemed to be mollified.

Virginia finished with the washing up and rushed to get her coat and scarf. She would never feel the same way about the rain, it was true, but it still made her just as wet when she had to tramp through it. She supposed it might spoil her noon shopping trip as well. Then she forced a smile. She would not allow it to spoil her day.

"Goodbye, Grandmother. I'll see you this evening. I must rush so I won't be late."

The woman turned her face up for a kiss and patted Virginia's arm. "It is so nice to have you here with us, dear," she said. "So nice for me and Jonathan."

Virginia almost winced. It was as though the older woman was making them a trio, rather than seeing Jonathan and Virginia as a pair.

But later, thoughts of her new husband brought a smile back as Virginia faced the wind and wetness. She had hurried to the cellar to pick herself an apple from the bushel basket. But feeling its smooth coolness in her pocket as she hurried to her job, she remembered that she had forgotten to cut herself a piece of cheese.

———

By the time Virginia got her lunch break, the rain had stopped, so she was able to leave her coat behind when she went out to do her shopping. The sun was now shining brightly, causing little shimmers of steam to rise up from the ground. The wind also had changed to a soft breeze, and fingers of sunshine reached down to caress Virginia's shoulders and face as she hurried from shop to shop for what she needed for the special supper.

Though she had visited the elderly woman often and helped with housework on more than one occasion, she had little idea what Mrs. Withers' cupboards contained. So to make sure she would be missing nothing, Virginia mentally went over each ingredient for the dishes she planned to prepare for Jonathan. She supposed there would be some basics already on hand, but being sure was better than finding herself without an item.

She was in a happy mood as she headed back to the post office. She would only need to stop by the butcher's on her way home and pick up the chicken for frying. She would have to work quickly if she was to have the pie baked and the chicken sizzling in the pan, the biscuits hot and ready and the potatoes whipped by the time Jonathan arrived. But she was sure she would manage, provided that Jonathan did not surprise them and come home early.

The post-office entry was never scrubbed more quickly than it was at the end of that Monday. Virginia grabbed her coat, picked up her bags of groceries, and started off for home, her cheeks warm in her excitement. Her first meal for her new husband. She would make him proud.

CHAPTER 5

The first thing Virginia noticed as she hurried up the walk was the smell of baking bread.

"Grandmother Withers has been busy," she observed with a smile on her way around to the back of the house. She tapped on the door. "Hello," she called softly as she had always done. "It's me."

She heard a chuckle even before her name was called. "Virginia, come in, dear. My, you don't have to stop to knock. You live here now."

Virginia moved into the steaming kitchen. Now she smelled a roast cooking. She looked around the room. Yes. This *was* her home now. She lived here with Jonathan and his grandmother—at least for the time being. Maybe the cooked food would keep. . . .

"I forget," she joked. But she lowered her parcels onto the kitchen table a bit uncertainly.

"Looks like you've been shopping," Grandmother Withers observed.

Virginia shrugged out of her coat as she answered slowly, "Yes. For supper. I was thinking I'd—"

"Supper? Supper is already on, dear," Grandmother Withers interrupted, waving a hand toward the stove. "I've even baked a fresh batch of bread. Never baked much when I was here alone. Just went stale with no one to eat it but me. But it's rather nice to have reason to cook again."

Virginia looked from the cooking pots on the stove to Grandmother Withers and back again. She wanted to protest, but she closed her lips tightly.

"Jonathan does love fresh bread. And roast. Always liked roast. Thought I'd fix him his favorites."

"That's . . . that's thoughtful," Virginia managed to say. It would be *her* supper that would have to keep.

"You have shopped?"

Virginia mutely nodded again.

"That's nice. You can shop and I'll cook. That'll work just fine."

Virginia nodded again. It really wasn't much fun to shop. One did not get compliments from one's husband for lugging in armloads of groceries.

"I bought chicken," she said. "Is there room in the icebox?"

"I think we can squeeze it in there. Jonathan likes chicken. Roasted with my special dressing."

"I . . . I bought frying chicken," admitted Virginia.

At first Mrs. Withers seemed to have to think about that. Then she smiled and patted Virginia's arm. "That's fine, dear. You'll know for next time."

Virginia shifted around some items to make room for the chicken and began to unload the rest of her purchases. Grandmother Withers stood at her elbow, her eyes shining like a child's at Christmas. "My, you *have* shopped," she enthused. "Cooking will be a pleasure with such a well-stocked cupboard."

Virginia knew she should be pleased with Grandmother Withers' response, but all she could feel at the moment was keen disappointment. Her supper would not be bringing a smile to the eyes of Jonathan after all.

————

As it turned out, Jonathan was late for supper. He came in, an apology ready on his lips, eyes seeking forgiveness. It was to Grandmother Withers that he said, "I am so sorry, Grandma. One of the mares is down. She is one of the best I have, so it's important to try to save her. I think there's something the matter with the foal she's carrying. Maybe the trip out was too much for her. I've done everything I know. I think I'll try to get a call through to Danny. He might be able to give me some advice."

Virginia, miffed because of his lateness and then hurt by his seeming to ignore her very presence, felt immediately contrite as she saw the deep concern on his face.

"Eat something first," Grandmother Withers was saying. "Then you can go and do what you need to do."

"Why don't you go on over to the folks'," suggested Virginia. "They'll help you reach Danny. They know a few of his study haunts. He's hardly ever in his dorm room. Says it's too noisy there."

Jonathan smiled his thanks and moved to his grandmother. "But I am sorry, Grandma. Supper smells wonderful. Sorry I've held you up. You should have eaten. If this happens again, please don't wait. You and Virginia go ahead and eat." He leaned over to kiss her snowy head.

"I knew it would be something important to hold you

up," Grandmother Withers assured him. "Go wash up. I'll dish up your plate."

Jonathan may have wanted to do things differently. But after a pause he crossed to the corner basin and vigorously scrubbed his work-hardened hands. He was drying them on the towel when he turned to Virginia. "How did your day go?"

Virginia found it hard to answer, but she managed a wobbly smile. She had been looking forward to Jonathan's embrace. His kiss—even on the top of her head.

I missed you, she longed to say. *I could hardly wait for you to get home, and then when you were late I was afraid. I don't know what I was afraid of. I just feared that you . . . that something might have happened.* But Virginia said only, "Fine."

"Good," he responded and turned to hang up the towel.

The meal was a rather silent one. Jonathan made a few attempts at conversation, but Virginia could tell that his thoughts were still on the ailing mare. She wished there were some way she could reach out and share his burden, but she could not think of anything meaningful.

"Virginia and I have already worked out our system," Mrs. Withers said cheerily.

"System?"

"In the kitchen. She will shop and clean up and I will do the cooking."

Jonathan said, "That's great! No reason she should come home at night and have to cook. But don't go spoiling her, Grandma. We won't always have the luxury of a live-in cook, you know."

He gave Virginia a wink and a smile that made her heart do a flip. Even Grandmother's new system could not dash her spirits when Jonathan looked at her that way.

He reached under the table and gave her hand a gentle squeeze. Virginia swallowed, her face flushing slightly.

When Jonathan's hand moved back, it gently brushed across her lap. Virginia's face felt very warm. Was Grandmother Withers aware of what was happening under her tablecloth? Virginia cast a quick glance her way and saw that the elderly woman was totally absorbed in cutting her roast. Virginia gave Jonathan a quick glance and saw the glint in his eyes.

"I'll make this as fast as I can," he told the two women as he rose from the table.

"There's apple pie," his grandmother informed him. "Sit down until you've eaten proper. Virginia, cut him a slice. We can have ours at leisure."

Virginia arose to do as bidden.

Jonathan sat back down, but Virginia could tell he was anxious to contact Danny and get back home to her.

When he had wolfed down the pie and was reaching for his broad-brimmed hat, he said he was off to make his call but would be right back. Virginia wanted to go with him, but she knew she should do the clean-up chores.

She was halfway through the dishes when he came in again, still agitated and preoccupied with the mare. "Managed to get hold of Danny. He thinks it might ease her if I . . . Well, no use bothering you ladies with all that. If the foal is dead she shouldn't be carrying it. Danny thinks it's likely that's her problem. I'm going back on out to see what I can do."

Virginia felt like protesting but she knew better; the horses were to be their means of livelihood. It was important that this mare be saved.

Jonathan did kiss her then. As she stood with her hands in the dishpan, Grandmother Withers seated at the kitchen table, he walked up behind her and slipped his arms around her waist. "So sorry, sugar," he whispered into her ear. "Don't wait up. I've no idea how long I'll be." Then he kissed her on the neck, making warm shivers pass the full length of her spine. But she could not even turn to him and wrap her arms around his neck in return. Her hands were all dishwater wet, and she felt far too self-conscious in the presence of his grandmother. "I'll be back, Mrs. Lewis," he whispered in her ear just before he turned to go.

Virginia had a hard time not adding tears to her dishwater as she heard the door close firmly behind her. She had the feeling it was going to be a long, lonely evening, even with the company of her new grandmother.

———

Virginia tried to pass the evening in companionship, but her thoughts kept going to Jonathan. When would he be home? Would he be able to save his prize mare? What would it mean to them if he could not? Jonathan had counted on the foal to bring a good price the next spring. At this stage, every foal was important.

"Do you knit?" Grandmother Withers' words interrupted her thoughts.

"Yes," answered Virginia, who had been trying desperately to make her mind concentrate on a book.

"That's good." Grandmother Withers did not explain why.

"Sew?"

"Yes." Virginia squirmed on her seat and turned another page.

"Good. Crochet?"

"Some."

"Lots of nice crochet patterns. I'd be glad to teach you some in the evenings."

"Thank you," responded Virginia.

"Quilt?"

Virginia shifted again, not sure where all the questions were leading.

"I've done some."

"Braided rugs?"

"Yes."

Mrs. Withers nodded her head approvingly. "We'll have lots of things to do together in the evenings," she said, sounding satisfied. "I missed all that with Damaris, you know. I often thought what it would be like to sit and work together. I was so lonely when Damaris left, but not sorry that she did. You understand. She had to go. It was the only thing that she could have done. And now we are too many miles apart to share those mother-daughter things. It'll be so nice to have you to do things with. Sort of make up for all of those years missed."

Mrs. Withers gave Virginia a smile filled with love, and Virginia answered with one of her own. It must have been so lonely for the poor woman. Virginia knew the story of Jonathan's mother, Damaris, leaving home as a young girl and fleeing west on her own to escape a drunken father. Virginia thought of all of the things she had been able to talk over with her mother, all the meals they had prepared together over the years, and suddenly she felt very blessed. "That will be nice," she assured Grandmother Withers. "What should we work on first?"

"You choose. Maybe a quilt, seeing how you'll need one when winter sets in."

Oh, but I already have quilts, Virginia could have stated. *Grandma and Mama saw to that.* But she did not say the words. Just smiled. "I'll get the material" was what she said instead.

When Grandmother Withers announced that she was

heading off to her bed, Virginia was only too happy to follow suit. She took her book with her, intending to read until she heard Jonathan return.

It was hard to concentrate on the words when all her thoughts were with Jonathan. Virginia turned pages, then turned back to reread what she had just perused. Nothing seemed to be registering. She shifted her weight this way and that, plumped pillows, then punched them flat. Nothing helped.

At last Virginia gave up. Her eyelids were so heavy she could hold them open no longer. She did not even turn off the lamp. Jonathan would be coming, and he'd need to find his way.

The next thing Virginia knew she was being kissed on the tip of the nose. When she opened her eyes she found Jonathan leaning over her, a lazy smile tilting his lips. "You look so sweet when you're sleeping," he whispered. "I could hardly make myself wake you up."

"Are you just getting to bed?" Virginia asked, blinking sleep-filled eyes.

He laughed in response. "No, sugar. It's another day."

Virginia pushed up onto an elbow and looked at the window behind her. Sure enough, the world outside was washed with morning sun.

"It's morning already?"

Jonathan laughed softly.

"Did you get any sleep at all?" Virginia wondered with concern.

"I did. Oh, not much, but at least enough to get me through another day."

"How's the mare?"

"I think we've made it. She lost the foal. But I think that, thanks to Danny, I have saved the mare."

Virginia knew that though the news was better than it could have been, it also was not good news. "You were

68

counting on that foal, weren't you?"

He leaned over farther and drew her into his arms. "I was. But when you're raising stock, you know better than to count too much on any one thing. Hopefully she will live to bear more foals." Then he said, "Now, how about a good-bye kiss?"

"Good-bye? You're just saying hello."

He chuckled softly. "Well . . . sort of. But I am also saying good-bye. I should have been out to the farm long ago. Grandma fixed my breakfast. I think she rather enjoys fussing over me." He wrinkled his nose and grinned.

I'd enjoy having a chance to fuss over you too, thought Virginia, but she quickly put aside all such thoughts as she was being thoroughly kissed.

"Will you be late again?" she asked when Jonathan allowed her to catch her breath.

"I don't know. I could be. Don't wait supper for me. No need for you and Grandma to endure empty stomachs."

Jonathan, it is not my stomach that concerns me, Virginia wanted to protest. *It's you I miss—not the supper*. But she said nothing, just clung to him as he kissed her again.

"Sorry to waken you so early, but I couldn't bear the thought of not saying good-bye before I left. Lay back down and catch a few more winks. You don't have to be up for another hour or so."

But Virginia was not able to go back to sleep after the bedroom door closed on Jonathan's tall figure. She lay there, staring at the door, wishing he could have stayed or she could have gone with him. That they could be together.

At last she gave up and crawled from the bed. She dressed slowly, deep in thought as she slipped on her blouse and skirt. Surely with the mare better Jonathan would not need to stay as late at the farm. Surely he would be able to come home at a decent hour and get some much-needed rest.

When she entered the kitchen, Mrs. Withers sat at the table, her Bible opened before her. "You're up early," she said with a smile.

Virginia nodded. "I couldn't sleep."

"I told Jonathan that he should leave you be, but oh no. He had to go and wake you up."

"I'm glad he did," Virginia was quick to assure the older woman. "I would have been miserable all day if I'd not even been able to tell him good-bye."

The woman nodded her head, then went back to her reading. "The porridge is on the back of the stove," she said without looking up.

"Thank you," replied Virginia, but she had absolutely no intention of choking down another bowl of morning porridge.

CHAPTER 6

$\mathscr{T}$he days fell into a kind of routine. Jonathan always woke a sleepy Virginia to bid her good-bye even before the dawn had broken. Virginia then rose and dressed for work, washed up from breakfast, and tidied the rest of the house. She usually left for the post office early enough that it meant a leisurely stroll. There was no reason to delay leaving the house; Jonathan was not there.

The mare did live, Virginia was thankful to learn. The prized animal would be able to contribute to the income of the farm in subsequent years. She shared Jonathan's disappointment about the foal, but they were both relieved not to lose the mare as well.

But Jonathan was working long hours out at the farm. Besides all the care for the stock, he had begun building the house that was to be their home. Virginia longed for a place of their own at the same time she was lamenting the work that kept Jonathan from her all day and often well into the night.

Be patient, she kept telling herself. *Just for a short time, and then we'll be able to have a normal home and life together— just the two of us.*

A normal home. Virginia was not exactly sure what that might be. She assumed it would be much like the one in which she had been raised—two folks caring for each other, doing things together, sharing a common faith and similar goals. Showing love and devotion toward each other. At the same time, Virginia reminded herself that her own father was gone for much of the day. He did not spend his time sitting around holding her mother's hand or stroking her brow. How was it they seemed to have such an easy understanding of each other's needs? Why was her mother so perfectly content just knowing that her father would be home "later"? Why did romance seem to matter so little and commitment seem to matter so much? Virginia thought that there must be a lot that she did not understand about the marriage relationship. All she knew, all she felt with every part of her being, was her intense longing to be with Jonathan. To have his full time and attention. To have him telling her with eyes and lips and arms just how much he adored her. Wasn't that why he had asked her to marry him? Wasn't that what marriage was all about? That total giving of one to the other?

Yet Jonathan seemed to be content. Though too busy. Too pressured. Too burdened with all the responsibilities. But content nonetheless. He came in late, ate a warmed-over supper, looked about to fall asleep on the kitchen chair, then was up again before the sun the next morning, ready to do it all over again. Virginia sometimes had the fleeting thought that she might as well pack up her bags and move on back to her old bedroom. *I wonder just how long it would take before I would be missed?* she mused, not totally facetiously.

But all of those rather mournful thoughts were laid aside when Jonathan came home. The feel of his arms as he pulled her close, the brush of his kiss against her temple—these alone were enough to make the long, lonely hours well worth the wait for his return. And when he whispered words of love all wrapped up with progress reports on the home he was building, Virginia scolded herself and repeatedly vowed to never fret inwardly again.

But it was hard to keep her silent promise. Especially when most of the few precious moments they had to share were not spent alone. Jonathan's grandmother seemed to always have a list of odd jobs for Jonathan, a jack-of-all-trades. "Men need to feel needed," Mrs. Withers confided to Virginia one evening as she sent Jonathan off with a post maul to pound in some stakes for her giant gladiolas. Virginia felt a lump growing in her throat; she needed Jonathan far more than those gladiolas did.

But Virginia knew it was useless to agitate against the circumstances. They had discussed the living arrangements before the wedding. She had agreed, fully agreed, that she would sooner spend some time sharing a home with Grandmother Withers than to have to wait for marriage until the farmhouse was built. Jonathan had been more than fair in leaving her with the final decision. He had warned her that it would take his time and attention to get the house ready for occupancy. It was not Jonathan's fault that she had not fully understood just how difficult it would be.

She and Grandmother Withers made quilts. Not just one, but three. In the evenings while waiting for Jonathan to return, they quilted together. It was not Virginia's chosen way to spend an evening. She would have been far happier with a good book. But Grandmother Withers seemed to enjoy the time, so Virginia endured. It did help to fill the long hours.

Virginia did not walk across the yard next door to her old home often. For one thing, she did not want her mother to guess just how lonely she was feeling. If they were to spend more than five minutes in each other's company, Belinda was sure to pick up on the fact. Virginia contented herself with a wave of the hand and a cheery "hello" across the back fence and an occasional Sunday dinner when all three were invited to the table.

In turn, Virginia asked permission to prepare dinners for her family. After all, it was Grandmother Withers' kitchen. It was not an easy chore as the kitchen was small and the table so crowded. But they did share a few such Sundays, laughing at the tight squeeze as they crowded in close to one another. Jonathan was always quick to say that things would be different when the farm home was completed, and then he would follow that with an up-to-the-minute report on his progress. Virginia felt as if they barely inched along from "the cellar hole is dug" to "the foundation is laid" to "the outer walls are framed" and then to "the roof joists are up." The house still had no inner walls, doors, or windows, and the summer was nearly over.

But Jonathan seemed pleased with each bit of news he had to tell the group about their home-to-be. Virginia supposed that was what mattered. After all, he knew far more about building than she did. Perhaps the inside of the house would materialize much more quickly once the outer construction was done.

———

Virginia opened her eyes to sunshine and Jonathan already pulling on his boots. His bare back was toward her for he had not yet put on his shirt and tucked it into his trousers. She stirred onto one elbow and pushed back her hair. He looked around.

"I thought you were still sleeping," he said, turning to face her fully.

"I was, until this very minute."

"You don't have to go to work today. I thought you would sleep in."

"My sleepiness left me."

He leaned over and drew her to him. "I have to get out to the farm," he said between kisses.

"Let me come with you." The sudden inspiration made Virginia struggle from his embrace so she could hasten from the bed.

"Come with me? What would you do for an entire day at the farm? There isn't even a decent place to sit out there."

"There must be a log or two with all that building," responded Virginia cheerily as she began to rummage in her drawer for appropriate clothes.

"What about Grandma?"

Virginia turned to face him. "What about Grandmother?" she repeated.

"She'd be all alone . . . for the entire day."

"Jonathan, as soon as the house is built she will be alone each day."

Her words only made him look solemn. "I've been thinking about that." But he did not explain more. Instead he said, "She wanted that back flower bed weeded today. I thought since you enjoy the flowers you would help her with it."

"I can do it Monday after work. It's not a big bed."

"She won't leave it alone—you know that. She'll go and try to do it herself."

"Well, you tell her to leave it for me. She always listens

to you. If you say that I'll do it on Monday, she'll be happy with that."

Jonathan said nothing, but he did not seem pleased, as she had expected he would, that she intended to go to the farm with him. Didn't he want to share some time with her? Didn't he look forward to being alone together like she did?

"What's the matter?" she asked, wondering if she really wanted to hear his answer. "I thought you were anxious to get the work done. I can help you."

Jonathan shook his head. "I'm afraid it would be more of a hindrance than a help, Virginia," he said carefully.

Her eyes widened. "Hindrance?"

"I shouldn't have said hindrance. Distraction. *Distraction* is more like it. I just don't think that I could get as much done with you there."

"Why? What would I do to—"

"My mind wouldn't be on it in the same way," he cut in. "That's all. I would be too busy thinking about you."

"And you don't think about me as long as I am out of sight—is that it?"

"Of course I think about you."

"But not enough for it to cause any disturbance of your work?"

Her voice had risen with a shrillness that neither of them were accustomed to hearing. He stood to his feet and tucked in his shirt, then snapped his suspenders into place over his shoulders.

"I . . . I don't know what you're saying," he began softly. "Please . . . let's not have a misunderstanding. What I meant is simply that—"

"What you mean is what you just said. You don't want me around because it might cause you to think about me, and that would be a . . . a disturbance."

"I didn't say anything about disturbance. That was your word."

"Nor did you deny it," Virginia threw back at him.

"I didn't deny it because in a way, it's true. Your presence on the building site might be disturbing. When I am dealing with heavy beams and boards, I need full concentration. If you were there, I doubt I could give it. I would be wondering if you were all right, if you were in any danger."

"Jonathan," said Virginia, her hands going to her hips and her breath coming in little gasps, "you have not given me your full concentration since the day I set foot in this house. The farm, the house, your grandmother—they all get far more of your attention than I do."

He looked stunned. Her words seemed to have reached him with full impact. Virginia could read in his face just how much pain they had inflicted. For one moment she felt triumph—glorious triumph. She did have his full attention now. He lifted one helpless hand toward her and started to say something, shook his head and thought better of it. The hand continued on up to brush at his hair, a gesture of frustration and defeat. Then he turned from her.

"I'm sorry," he said. That was all. Then he left, closing the door quietly behind him. Virginia supposed that he had done so out of consideration for his grandmother. She heard the outer back door close quietly as well. Any feelings of triumph seemed to have departed with him. She threw herself on the rumpled bed and wept.

————

"All married couples have little tiffs." Jenny's words came back to Virginia many times as she focused all her energy into routing the weeds from Grandmother Withers' back

flower bed. Well, at least Jonathan had not left her with a bruised cheek. His quiet "I'm sorry" still rang in her ears. No comeback, no argument, no defensiveness, no telling her to be reasonable. Just "I'm sorry." And he had truly sounded as though he was.

Virginia tore at the weeds and watered the garden with salty tears as she worked her way across the flower bed. She wished it were weedier. Bigger. She would be done before she knew it, and then what would she do with the rest of her day? She wished she were at the post office. At least then she would have something to occupy her thoughts and her hands. Perhaps there was some grocery shopping that needed to be done. No. She had done that yesterday. She could go have tea with her mother. No. Belinda would quickly perceive that something was wrong. Maybe Clara. Maybe Clara had a job that needed some help. No. Clara had said that she was taking the kids to the farm to see the great-grandparents. Virginia wished she had begged to go along.

What would she do with the long, lonely day? Jonathan was sure to work until there was no more light for pounding a nail. Then, with the help of the lantern, he would make one more round to be sure all the stock was safe and secure. Then it was the long trip home. Oh, not that long. Just long for one who was tired from a day of hard labor. Jonathan always came home sweaty and exhausted. Ready to fall into bed as quickly as possible.

From feelings of anger, Virginia's thoughts and emotions traveled on to shame. She'd had no right to lash out at Jonathan as she had. He was doing all he could to give her the home she wanted. He had warned her that it would take long hours. Many days. *But still*, she mourned, *isn't there some way he could give me a bit more of his time? His attention?*

Her words to him, however cruel and biting, had been

true. She had been feeling them for a long time. Trying to force them down, fight them back. It wasn't an accusation without foundation. But it had been unfair. It had been said in the wrong manner. Surely she could have discussed her feelings in a reasonable fashion. What if she had killed his love? What if he no longer cared to express his love even in those times when they were able to be together? She would die without Jonathan. Just wither and die. She loved him so much. Even when she was angry with him, as she was now, the thought of losing him was more than she could endure.

Virginia mentally worked her way through her problem from every angle and always came back to the same unwanted conclusion: She had acted like a shrew. *With plenty of reason*, she would quickly attempt to excuse herself. *But it was unkind, unlovely*, she would reproach herself again. Back and forth her troubled thoughts tumbled. On the one hand, there was no reason good enough for her to have acted as she did. To have spoken as she did. Jonathan was giving of his best—himself—for her. But Jonathan was not being fair to treat a new bride as though she barely existed. Jonathan paid far more attention to his aging grandmother than he did to her. Yet it was his caring and gentle spirit that had attracted her to him in the first place. Well, why didn't he have time to show her the same concern he showed others?

Virginia was having an inner argument that either way she would lose.

———

Virginia could not wait for the day to end, yet she dreaded its ending. She could not wait for Jonathan to come home, yet feared his coming. She fidgeted and fretted and paced about the kitchen until Grandmother

Withers said, "Is something wrong, dear?"

Virginia could not answer with a lie so she said nothing in reply.

"It's been a long day for you, hasn't it? It's always that way when one has extra time and no way to fill it. I know. I used to nearly go crazy for my Damaris on those days when I couldn't pour my heart and soul into my work. Sundays. I never allowed myself ordinary work on Sunday. But I had no church service to attend. No real understanding about why one went to church. Just a hanging on to the past. A knowledge that my mother and father felt that church was important. That the Sabbath, the day of rest, be honored. So I just lolled about on Sunday. Agitated and wishing the hours to end. I was so thankful to go off to bed knowing that the next morning would bring me more work than I could handle in a single day."

Virginia listened. She was relieved that the elderly woman did not understand what her real problem was. All the same, Virginia was more than thankful to retire early. Perhaps if she tried hard, she could be asleep by the time Jonathan returned home.

CHAPTER 7

$\mathcal{V}$irginia was awakened by Jonathan's arms drawing her close. She stirred, then snuggled against him, struggling for wakefulness and understanding. "Virginia," she heard his voice next to her ear, "we need to talk."

Virginia pulled back and tried to see his face in the darkness of their bedroom. "What is it?" she asked sleepily. "Are you all right?"

His arms tightened around her, drawing her close again. "Are you awake?"

She mumbled against his chest. Her body insisted that it was the middle of the night.

He kissed her forehead. "Go back to sleep," he said softly. "We'll talk tomorrow. We both need to be wide awake to sort this out."

Suddenly Virginia was jolted out of her dreamy state. Jonathan was back from the farm. They'd had a disagreement before he'd left. Somewhere deep inside she still felt anger and confusion. She tried to pull away again but his arms held her. "I'm awake," she said firmly, and this time she really was.

He was silent for what seemed to be a long moment; then she felt more than heard his deep sigh.

"I'm afraid I have been dreadfully selfish," he began. "I had missed you so much when I was out west and never wanted to be without you again. But it was wrong for me to ask you to marry me before the house was ready. Before I was established on the farm. We should have waited."

"But you said that might take months. Years," interjected Virginia.

"I expect it will."

"We never could have—would have—waited that long."

His arms tightened around her, and he pressed his cheek against her forehead. It was several minutes before he spoke again. "I hadn't realized how hard this has been for you. These months of being with Grandma."

"Jonathan, it is not your grandmother that's the problem here. I . . . I love her. As if she were my own. It's not seeing *you*. Never having you to myself. No . . . private times. How can a marriage grow if we aren't allowed to . . . to even get to know each other?"

Again he was silent.

"Being with you like this is enough for me . . . for now," he finally answered.

"Well, it's not enough for me." She put both hands on his chest and pushed. Jonathan released her.

She heard him sigh again as though he was deeply troubled. "What would be enough for you?" he dared to ask, his voice still gentle.

"Being able to be like a normal husband and wife. With time. Time to talk. Time to . . . enjoy each other. Time to care for the needs of the other. I don't even get to cook for you. Grandma makes your breakfast, fixes your lunch, gets supper."

"I didn't know that cooking was that important to you. I'm sure Grandma—"

"That's not the point."

"But . . ."

"I'm not being a wife. I'm just here . . . when you finally come home at night. Then you're gone again in the morning before I'm even up."

"Virginia, we talked about this before we were married. You knew. I tried to tell you how it would be. I thought you understood. . . ."

"I thought I did too, but I guess I didn't. Not really. I mean, these are supposed to be the . . . the honeymoon days. And we've missed them, Jonathan. Totally missed them."

"Totally?"

"Totally!"

"You haven't been happy?"

"I've been lonely."

"I'm sorry."

Only the hall clock's tick sounded in the quiet for a very long time.

He had not tried to take her back in his arms. His stillness and his silence frightened her. She would have felt much better, more secure, had he chosen to argue the points she was making.

At last he spoke, but still he did not move. "I've really messed it up, haven't I?"

It was Virginia who moved. She leaned toward him and slipped her hand up and over his shoulder, curling her fingers in the thickness of the hair at the back of his neck. "You haven't messed it up," she said, for the first time with contrition in her voice. "I was as anxious for our marriage as you were."

83

"So what do we do? How can we fix this?" His arm encircled her again.

Virginia felt hot tears as they streaked down her cheeks. She had no answer.

"We do need a house," he continued. "We do need the horses."

Silently Virginia agreed.

"I need you."

His arm tightened and Virginia's tears increased.

"I can't promise things are going to get any better," he admitted honestly.

The thought was scary, but Virginia knew she had to accept it.

"Can you . . . can you manage . . . somehow . . . for a few more months?"

"I'll have to." Virginia's voice trembled.

"Would you be happier . . . back home?"

The very thought made Virginia cringe. To go home would be to admit defeat. It would be saying to the world that they had made a mistake. That they weren't strong enough to see their commitment through. "No," she said with emphasis. "No. I don't want to go home."

"You want to bunk in the barn?" His voice was teasing.

"It's tempting."

He kissed her. First on the nose. Then on her forehead. "What are we gonna do?" he asked into her hair as he pulled her tightly to his chest.

Virginia felt tears again. She could not speak. Could not express all the mixed emotions whirling around inside her, making her feel both joy and sadness at the same time. All she could do was cling to him.

———

Their routine changed somewhat. Jonathan still got up before the sun and prepared to leave for the farm. But he brought his second cup of morning coffee to their small bedroom and with it a cup for Virginia. Sleepily she would prop herself up in the bed and sip until her mind cleared and she was able to talk. And they talked. Pointless conversation by many standards. But discussion about their daily lives that strengthened the bond of care and concern for each other and helped to bridge the miles and hours they were apart. Then Jonathan occasionally teased her about getting up to make his lunch, when she knew full well his grandmother had already placed it in the small sugar sack Jonathan carried to the farm.

Virginia made a greater attempt to stay awake until Jonathan came home at night, and if he was especially tired she rubbed his back and arm muscles with the vile-smelling linament from his grandmother's medicine cabinet. And they talked then too.

Virginia worked hard to fill the fall evenings with projects that would be needed in the new house. Grandmother Withers clucked and fussed and beamed her approval, seeming to enjoy every moment of having "a daughter" in the house. Virginia tried not to feel too confined and restricted. But there were times when she longed for a wee bit of solitude; if her hours could not be spent with Jonathan, she would have preferred to be mostly alone.

With fall closing in on winter, Jonathan was in even more of a hurry to get the building to the place where it could be heated so he could do the finishing work during the winter months. Virginia was taken out for the occasional Sunday tour. She approved of what she found, and it made her that much more anxious to be in a home of her own. A real wife. A real homemaker.

"Perhaps by Christmas," Jonathan promised, and Virginia mentally crossed off the "perhaps" and clung to hope.

In the meantime, she was marking time. Trying not to become impatient. Trying hard to be pleasant company for Grandmother Withers. Trying to be supportive and understanding of Jonathan. At times she felt that she walked through the entire day holding her emotions at bay. Like holding one's breath.

——————

Snow came earlier than Jonathan would have hoped. The house still did not have its chimney. There was no way he could heat the building without the chimney being in place. Without his saying the words, Virginia knew it worried him. She tried to be extra supportive, but she didn't know what to say that would take the frown of worry from his brow or the troubled look from his eyes. It was especially hard when Grandmother Withers chattered on about local happenings or a bench that needed a nail pounded in or a hinge that squeaked for oil. Virginia saw Jonathan fight for pleasantness and at times wished to hush the older woman and banish her to her room.

But there was no way she could protect Jonathan from the reality of the situation. She had to accept that. There was not even a way she truly could comfort him. And the new house seemed to have a will of its own—lagging behind Jonathan's projected times for a particular section, dragging its feet in advancement. Virginia chaffed inwardly but tried to smile outwardly. It was taxing. Without verbally agreeing, they stopped talking about it.

"So, Jonathan, how's the house coming?" Virginia's father posed the question at a family dinner. Jonathan and Virginia exchanged glances, and she held her breath. She had not heard a progress report for a number of days. She knew Jonathan would answer the query honestly. Now she was afraid that what she was about to hear would be terribly disappointing.

"It's slow," he said, buttering a slice of fresh bread.

"It's a shame we can't help you more."

Jonathan nodded. "If my time wasn't so taken up with the stock, I could have made use of more help with the building," he said frankly. "I have to spend a good share of my day working with the horses, so the house gets piecemeal attention. I could hardly ask family and friends to try to fit those hodgepodge hours. Nor could I expect them to keep on working while I went to break a yearling."

Drew nodded. His legal office kept him at his desk both long hours and off-hours.

Virginia had never been able to understand about the horses, about all the attention they required. Jonathan had tried to explain, but it had never made much sense.

"How are the horses?" This from her father again.

"Got some real promising yearlings. But they won't be of much value unless they're proper broke. Might as well buy you a mustang if it's not trained. These are spirited, so they need time and attention. I don't hold to the manner of breaking a horse's spirit in order to be in control. They're much better if they're gentle broke. That takes time. Lots of time. And patience. You need to work them some every day. I've got five at the moment, and it takes a good share of my day to just keep some progress on the breaking in."

"It has to be done now? Immediately?" asked Belinda, seeming not to understand any more than Virginia did.

"Now's the right time. If they are left to themselves any longer, they can pick up bad habits. Can get more determined. I've been handling these fellas since they were foals. They trust me at this point. Now's the time to work with them before they become too independent. Especially the young stallions, and I've got a couple of those in the lot."

Belinda nodded, seeming to fully accept Jonathan's words.

"Couldn't you just sell them and let the buyer break them?" This question from Francine.

"Could. But I'd lose a lot of money. Well-broke horse is worth five or six times what an unbroken horse is. No, Francine. If Virginia and I are going to make it raising horses, I've got to do the training."

Virginia did not miss the inclusion of her in the plans for the farm. It gave her an odd little thrill—though totally undeserved, she felt. She'd had nothing at all to do with any of the horses, save to hang over the rail fence and feed one or the other an occasional apple or handful of oats.

"Hopefully next spring there will be more foals to work with. That's good news for the future. But once you get behind, you never catch up. The little guys have to be halter broke and handled. Mostly just petted and pampered, used to having you around. The touching and gentling is important."

"Oh, I could do that," put in Francine, her eyes shining.

"I'm sure you could," responded Jonathan with a chuckle and a nod for the girl. "I might just call on you come next spring."

Francine looked pleased.

"That mare you were worried about—still doing okay?" Drew wondered.

"Right as rain. She gets friskier every day. Don't think I would have saved her without Danny's advice. Is he planning on being a vet around here?"

Drew shook his head. "I don't suppose so. Has these big dreams of working with exotic animals rather than just farm stock. Wants to work in a zoo or some big game farm or something."

"We sure could use him or someone like him around here. Lose one prime animal and it can cost you a lot of money. Sometimes the entire year's profits."

"I suppose so."

It sounded dreadfully risky to Virginia.

"Have you heard anything from Jenny?" Belinda changed the topic after a pause in the conversation. Virginia shook her head. There had been no word from Jenny over the several months since she had made her sudden appearance—and disappearance.

"Things must be going all right. At least I hope so. Otherwise we would likely have heard from her again. She knows she can come here if she . . ." Virginia let her words trail off. She had been about to say, *if she needs to get away from her husband.* Somehow that didn't seem to be the proper way to be speaking about a marriage.

"I do hope she is feeling better. She looked so weak and pale it broke my heart. And that poor child . . . Her eyes still haunt me."

Virginia knew the feeling. There were many days and even more nights when the eyes of the child would haunt her as well. Such a fragile, mournful little thing.

"I can't help but wonder what the future can hold for her," Belinda said, her voice low.

"It's painfully true, as the Scripture says, that the sins of the parents are burdens to the children." Drew, who had not seen Jenny or her little one during their short call, had taken Belinda's word for the state of their well-being. "Jenny has pushed God away for many years. It's a shame that the little one might bear the brunt of her rejection."

The words were sobering, and all those around the table fell into thoughtful silence.

Francine broke the spell. "You should see Anthony

throw the ball," she enthused about her little nephew. "He just about put out a window all the way from the back fence. Troy was playing with him, and he had no idea the little fellow could throw that hard."

All eyes and ears tuned in to the latest story of Clara's young son. It seemed quite natural that thoughts concerning the responsibility of parents to their children would turn to parents who were taking their role seriously—parents who adored their youngsters and sought God's help daily in leading them in the right way.

"Then Jeffy had to try to mimic his older brother. He has to do everything just like Anthony does. Only he could hardly get his tiny fingers around the ball. And when he threw it, he didn't quite know how to let go."

They all laughed, and the conversation turned to much cheerier things than delayed houses, ailing mares, or errant mothers.

Virginia was relieved. The dinner table talk had been rather depressing. She had been telling herself—and was almost convinced—that once the house was finished, things would change. Jonathan would suddenly have time. Time to be a husband. Time to learn to know his wife. Time for them to share and grow together. Now with the discussion of how much time the horses took, how important it was that they receive the proper training, it didn't seem like that time would ever arrive. Was that true? Was that how it would always be? Would Jonathan never have time to be a real husband?

The thought frightened Virginia. She had so longed for a real husband-wife relationship where things would be shared. Joys and struggles and talk and laughter. Now it was sounding like she would only have an absentee husband—someone to cook and clean for, like a hired hand.

But, no. That was silly. Even in the few moments that she and Jonathan were able to have together, there was so much love. So much devotion. If she had to choose, she would do it all over again. Marry her Jonathan just for those few moments of the day that she had him all to herself. But it was not easy. She was honest about that. Knowing and loving Jonathan as she did, she was conscious of how wonderful it would be if her dreams had worked out as she had expected. Oh, it would be glorious to have his time and attention most hours of the day.

Virginia lowered her head and blinked back tears. She would not be spoiling the family dinner.

———

Thankfully, Indian summer meant that the sun came out again, the snow melted, and Jonathan was able to apply himself to putting in the chimney at the farmhouse. Virginia was almost as thankful as he was when the task was finally completed. She was able to select the stove that she wanted in her kitchen, while Jonathan picked the heater for the upstairs rooms. The living room would be heated by a large fieldstone fireplace, which as yet had not been built.

However, the warm weather also meant that Jonathan was able to put in even longer days than usual. He'd work with the horses during the hours of sunshine, then move into the house to work by lamplight into the long, dark evenings.

Virginia said nothing. Soon, hopefully very soon now, they would have their own home. At least she would be close enough to Jonathan to catch glimpses of him from the window as he worked with the animals in the corral. There would be some comfort in that.

CHAPTER 8

Virginia smiled her welcome over the post-office counter. Sarah Thompson was three years her junior, and they had never been more than acquaintances in school, but the fact that they had married the same summer gave them some kind of kinship.

Sarah returned the smile along with a shy "Hello."

"I go past your house every day on my way to work. I love what you have done with the new bay window."

Sarah beamed. "That's Geoffrey. He's very good at carpentry. How's your house coming?"

"We hope to be in by Christmas."

"You must be really looking forward to that."

"I am. Some days I can hardly stand the wait," said Virginia truthfully.

"Well, Christmas isn't far away now. I can't believe how quickly it has come this year. When I was a youngster it seemed it would never arrive."

Sarah purchased two stamps for the letters she was posting and smiled again. She was turning to leave when the door opened.

Virginia knew the woman by sight only. She was fairly new to the town and lived in the house next to Sarah and her Geoffrey. Any time Virginia and she had chanced to meet, she seemed loud and vulgar, so Virginia had never sought to encourage a friendship. Now the woman greeted Sarah in a rough, husky voice, posted a letter, and rummaged through the mailbox assigned to her.

"See you got that new window in," she observed with her back to the younger woman.

"Yes. Geoffrey finished it last Thursday."

The woman turned slightly to look at the smiling face. "You seem mighty pleased with it."

"I am."

"And Geoffrey?"

"He's pleased too."

"I wasn't referring to your Geoffrey's carpentry skills. I was meaning your Geoffrey. You still enamored?"

The younger woman looked puzzled.

"So you haven't hit the stone wall yet?"

"I'm sorry. I . . . I don't understand."

"The stone wall, honey. The stone wall of reality. Every new bride hits it sooner or later. Sometimes it takes a while. Sometimes you hit it the first day."

"I don't know . . ."

The older woman's harsh, mirthless laugh intruded on Sarah's words. "Well, you haven't hit it yet—that's easy to tell. But you will. Mind me, you will. One of these days that shine will go from your eyes, and you'll realize all those fairy tales of happy-ever-after are just that—fairy tales. No man is as good as he looks at the altar. But who am I to tell you that? You'll find it out soon enough."

She gave the young woman a tap on the shoulder with

the curled paper she held in her hand. Then she laughed heartily, the same hollow laugh. "Enjoy it while you can," she said with another playful slap. Then she was gone.

Sarah cast one pleading look Virginia's way as though asking for someone to contradict the woman's statement, then left silently.

But the words seemed to hang heavily in the air around Virginia. Was there truth in what the woman said? Was there a time of reality when all young brides realized that fairy tales did not come true? That the knight in shining armor was nothing more than a fellow human full of faults, foibles, and weaknesses? Were her expectations of marriage unrealistic? Had her dreamlike vision of love been totally impossible to live up to—both for Jonathan and for herself? The thoughts troubled her for the remainder of the day.

―――――

"Clara . . . have you ever hit the stone wall?"

Clara stopped slicing the raisin loaf and turned to look at Virginia, her eyes puzzled and curious. "Stone wall? What stone wall?"

"I don't know . . . exactly. I overheard a discussion in the post office yesterday, and one woman insisted that every bride, sooner or later, hits the stone wall. "Of reality," she said. When you realize that marriage is not a fairy tale."

"Oh," said Clara and continued to slice the loaf.

When there was no further comment, Virginia pressed. "Is it true?"

"I wouldn't know," said Clara. "I've only been one bride."

"But . . . did you?"

Clara turned with the plate of sliced bread. "Have I hit

the stone wall of reality? That's not an easy question, Virginia."

"What do you mean, not easy?" Virginia asked, her tone impatient. "I would think you would know whether it has happened to you or not."

Clara took her place at the table and began to pour their tea. "Well, it all depends on how hard you have to hit the wall," she said as she set the teapot on the table and put the cozy back in place to keep it warm.

Virginia's eyes stared at Clara's face. She was becoming more and more impatient.

"I suppose, to one degree or another, there comes a time when a woman—or a man, I'd imagine, but I won't speak for them—realizes that marriage is—is more than the first blush of romance. Reality—life, if you will—has many demands on both the man and the woman. You have to face that. Sit down and take stock, if you know what I mean."

It sounded cold, calculating, to Virginia. Not one bit romantic.

"We live in a world that demands our time and attention. I think that is even more true for the man than the woman. He is expected to provide a home, make a living, care for the needs of the family. And if he is at all worth his salt, he takes those needs seriously. We need to realize and respect that.

"For us, who are more romantic creatures, sometimes we struggle with understanding. With finding the right balance. It is easy to miss the intent and just judge the actions."

"What do you mean?"

"Well, take Troy. I hate to use personal experience, but it's the only one I am familiar with. I . . . I wouldn't want to make you think that I'm not satisfied with Troy. He's a wonderful husband. A wonderful father."

Virginia wished to tell Clara to just get on with her explanation.

"There was a time when I thought Troy was spending far too much time at his father's store. I couldn't understand why he wouldn't rush right home and take me in his arms every day."

"He didn't?"

"No, he didn't. In fact, at one point I accused him of purposely dawdling."

"You didn't!"

"I did—to my shame."

"How long had you been married?"

"About six months."

"Did you have a spat?"

Clara hesitated, then continued. "We did. One jolly good round."

"Did it. . . ? Did he change?"

"I'm not sure. But I know I did."

"You did?"

"I decided, after prayer and tears, to grow up, Virginia."

"Grow up?"

"I was acting like a child. Wanting his full attention. His declarations of love. I wanted to be his little princess, I guess. The one he worshiped and adored. Well, life's not like that. And after thinking it through, I actually wouldn't want it to be. We aren't put together in a marriage to stroke each other's ego. Marriage is a partnership. A blending of two lives. A working together. That's where the commitment comes in. It's a determination of the head—not the heart. No, I shouldn't say it that way. It still involves the heart. It still is based on love, but it's a new kind of love. A mature love. One that doesn't ask, 'What will you do for me?' but rather, 'What can I do for you?' or 'What can we do for each other?' It gives meaning to love. To the whole marriage relationship."

Virginia sat and thought about the words.

"So it doesn't bother you anymore if Troy is late?"

Clara laughed. "Sure it does. Sometimes I'm still tempted to tell him so. But I understand now more about *why* he is late. I am more confident now in his love. His real love. Not just the flutter of heartbeats at the excitement of a stolen kiss."

Virginia thought of the evening before when Jonathan had sneaked a kiss when his grandmother's back was turned. Her heart had beaten faster with the thrill of it.

Virginia stirred. "So you are saying that every new bride does hit the stone wall?"

"I don't think it's as drastic as hitting a wall, Virginia. I've heard the expression 'The honeymoon is over.' Haven't you?"

Virginia nodded, then said somberly, "I didn't get a honeymoon."

"I know. That's a shame. But personally, I don't think they are essential. A trip later, when you know each other better and don't have to sort through—"

"No. I mean, I didn't get a honeymoon time. Period."

Clara looked at her thoughtfully.

"There's never been a honeymoon time for Jonathan and me," Virginia explained. "We've always had his grandmother there—with us in the room or asking Jonathan for his help or fussing over him. She cooks all his favorite foods and makes sure that his Sunday shirt is starched just so. Even at night . . . in our little bedroom, I fear that the walls are . . . are far too thin. I don't even dare start—start an argument for fear she'll be listening." Virginia couldn't help but chuckle at her own words, and Clara joined her.

Sobering, Clara said, "I hadn't realized . . ."

"It's been like that ever since the first day of our married life."

"Well, you will soon be in your own home, and then . . ."

"We can't go back and find those first lost days, Clara. They're gone. We can never reclaim them."

Clara toyed with her cup. "Yes," she said at last. "They are gone, and that's a shame. And I think you're right. You can't go back to the beginning. The relationship has moved beyond that now. It will never again have the newness, the innocence of the beginning. But you can start where you are, Virginia. Maybe you've got a head start on that."

"How?"

"By learning from where you have been. By trying to understand how it has been for Jonathan."

"Jonathan says that . . . that what he's had has been enough to make him happy. He's perfectly content to work at the farm all day and come home tired at night to a tiny room where we can scarcely turn around."

"Good!"

"Good?"

"You must be doing something right. Start there."

"I'm not doing anything. Not even cooking his meals."

"Why do you keep coming back to this meal business? Do you think all Jonathan thinks about is food?"

"No. I . . . I guess it's just . . . symbolic of caring for him, or something."

"And do you know what Jonathan sees as symbolic of caring for you? Building your house. Giving you shelter. That's the expression of his love. And he won't rest until it's done. He's driven to provide for you, Virginia. Until you are in that new home, Jonathan will feel a failure.

He'll feel that he has not expressed his love to you like he should."

Virginia shook her head, tears brimming in her eyes. "Oh boy. If he only knew that I'd trade all the new houses in the world for his time."

" 'Time' can get a little chilly on a winter's night. Real love is more practical than that."

They sat in silence for a few moments. "This tea is cold as rainwater." Clara moved to pour out the objectionable beverage and returned for a fresh cup.

"I've been impatient with Jonathan," Virginia admitted frankly.

"We all make mistakes."

"He's been so sweet it hurts."

Clara reached out and took Virginia's hand. "You've got a good man, little sister. Hang on to him. Make him happy."

Virginia nodded through her tears. "It still grieves me to think that we missed the fun, exciting honeymoon part," she whispered, her chin trembling.

When Clara did not speak, Virginia went on. "I didn't even get the courting. The flowers. The candy. Those long moonlit walks. The . . ."

"I'm sorry. You did miss a special time. But it was your choice."

"I know . . . but I guess I miss it. That special feeling that . . . I guess I didn't understand how it would be."

"But you've got the best part ahead."

Virginia could not feel sure. "You think I've hit the wall?"

"No. Only if you let it be a wall. You've come to a turning point. A decision-making time. Many couples flounder when the marriage reaches that point. But it's a decision, Virginia. A choice you get to make. What are you going to do with a real marriage? Not a fairy tale. A real marriage. Are you going to throw your heart and soul into it and, with God's help, build a happy and stable home with the man you love? Or are you going to retreat, still wanting to be the little princess on an imaginary throne? You can't have it both ways."

"But I love romance."

"Romance? That's when true romance begins. That's when you learn to appreciate romance for what it really is. That's the real beginning—not the end. You get so busy looking for ways to show love that your whole day becomes one exciting opportunity."

Virginia's eyes widened, and she stared at her sister. "You still love Troy . . . like that?"

"Still? No, not still. I love Troy more now than I ever have before. More than I ever did when I was going all giddy over his little love notes or our carved initials on a tree."

"But the honeymoon time. . . ?"

"I love him more than that too. I see him now, carrying in groceries, fixing downspouts, shoveling snow from the walks. I watch him listen to the boys' evening prayers, see him teach them how to hit a ball. I feel his concern about my tired back at the end of a day as he reaches out to massage away the ache, see in his eyes his love for this new baby—the one he doesn't even know yet. Those are the things that I love about Troy. Those and many, many more."

Virginia straightened and dabbed at her eyes with her hankie. "I think I'm beginning to understand," she said quietly. "I'm glad we had this little chat."

Clara squeezed the hand she still held.

———

"I have a Christmas present for you," Jonathan whispered to Virginia as he joined her beneath the feather quilt. She forced sleep from her foggy brain and tried to raise herself to a sitting position.

"What?" she asked sleepily.

"A new house?" His voice ended the statement like a question.

Virginia came fully awake. "You mean. . . ?"

"It's not totally finished. I'll have to keep working on it as we go, but if you like, we can move in. It's far enough along to be livable. If . . . you don't mind putting up with that—for a while."

"But I thought . . ."

"Your grandpa Clark has been helping me. We wanted it to be a surprise."

Did she mind? Would she put up with an unfinished house? There was no doubt in her mind. They would be together. They would be alone. It was an answer to her prayers.

"Oh, Jonathan."

Virginia threw herself into his arms. But it was tears that came rather than laughter. She wasn't sure, but in the darkness she wondered if there were tears on his cheeks too.

CHAPTER 9

$\mathscr{I}$t was neither large nor fancy. There were no bay windows. No winding staircases. The structure was plain and solid. The simple floor plan was designed for practicality. As yet there was no trim around the doors and windows. No finishing paint or wallpaper on the walls. Yet Virginia could not have imagined the excitement she felt upon moving into her very own home. It was like every Christmas, every birthday, every picnic—and the first time Jonathan said he loved her—all rolled into one. Jonathan watched and chuckled. Then shook his head, by turn. He'd had no idea just how much having her own place would mean to her.

"Oh, I can't wait to bake bread," she enthused as she ran a hand lovingly over the surface of the new stove's gleaming enamel oven door. Then she rushed about making up beds, hanging temporary curtains, spreading out rugs.

"Just think. I can unpack all the dishes. They have a cupboard now."

And on and on she went, savoring every minute of the new experience.

That evening when Jonathan came in from his final chores, Virginia handed him a mug of hot chocolate and beckoned to him to join her by the fireplace. Together they sipped and chatted as the fire crackled in the hearth, and the sound of an occasional whinny was the only intrusion from the outside night.

"You must be exhausted," Jonathan observed.

"I am a little weary, but it's a good tired. I like this kind of work much better than any old post-office job," she noted, inwardly thankful once again that she had been able to quit when they moved.

"I guess your 'nesting' is much like my building. Tired doesn't count."

Virginia shook her head to clear her thinking and stared at the fireplace flames. Was that how it had been for Jonathan? Was his eagerness to get the home built similar to her eagerness to actually move in and live there? No wonder he often had not come back until the middle of the night.

"I still have more to do tomorrow," Virginia said, turning to him, "but I'm amazed at how much I was able to get done today."

Jonathan's eyes roamed the room. "It looks real homey," he observed.

"It does, doesn't it? It feels homey too." She moved from her chair to sit at his feet and lean her head against his knee. "Jonathan, I can't tell you how happy I am. Almost like we're . . . we're starting fresh. . . ." She didn't explain further, but Jonathan's hand stroked her hair in unspoken response.

Virginia lifted her head to gaze again at her new surroundings. "Do you suppose you might find time tomorrow to get us a Christmas tree?"

Jonathan nodded. "Where're you going to put it?"

"In the corner by the window."

"Got any do-bobs for it?"

"Do-bobs?"

"You know. To hang on it. Fancy it up."

"Decorations? No. But I'll make some."

"That'd be nice. But it's only three days till Christmas."

"Oh, I'll manage," she said lightly. Then, "I wish . . . I wish we hadn't promised the folks that we'd have Christmas with them. It would be fun to have it here, in our new house."

"Guess we'll have lots of Christmases here."

Virginia nodded. Lots of Christmases. Their whole life stretched before them with open-ended promise.

Jonathan set aside his empty mug. "Do you have to wash it up tonight?" he asked Virginia.

She shook her head slowly, puzzled at his question. "It can wait for morning."

"Good."

He stood to his feet. " 'Cause I'm sure anxious to see how you've set up our bedroom."

Virginia flushed and stretched her hand to reach his, and he pulled her to her feet.

———

Their Christmas celebration with the family included Grandpa Clark and Grandma Marty as well as Grandmother Withers.

"My, I've been missing you something awful," the elderly lady said in greeting as she gave Virginia a tight hug.

"As soon as the weather warms up, Jonathan will be in

to get you and bring you out to see the house," Virginia promised. "We even have a spare bed so you can stay the night."

"Oh, I don't know if I should do that. Fires need to be tended in this kind of weather."

"We'll find someone to check your fires. I'm sure Father—"

"Wouldn't want my indoor plants to freeze. That new violet is blooming now. You should see it. Prettiest thing I've ever seen. Deep blue with a light blue fringe."

"It sounds lovely."

Virginia moved on to greet her grandparents.

"Hear you've got a right nice little place out there," said Marty. Virginia only nodded, but her eyes were shining with her joy.

From her grandmother's embrace she moved to her grandfather. "I understand you had a hand in helping get us in by Christmas," she said, hugging Clark close.

"Well, now, I didn't do much. Your man did the lion's share of the work. You got yourself a good one, my dear."

"I know, Grandpa," said Virginia, turning to give Jonathan a proud smile.

"I'm anxious to see it," put in Marty.

"New Year's," said Virginia, nodding enthusiastically. "Jonathan and I have talked it over, and we'd like to invite the family for New Year's dinner. Can you come?"

All agreed they would have a New Year's dinner and a housewarming, in one event. Virginia thought her heart would burst with emotion.

———

Before they scarcely had time to let the Christmas turkey settle, the sun was dipping toward the western horizon. People began searching out heavy coats and hats and scarves, bundling up against the chill of winter. Jonathan signaled to Virginia with a slight nod, and she, too, went to get their wraps. They faced a cold drive. Virginia was anxious to get home so she could stretch out her feet toward the fire and sip a cup of hot apple cider. And look around again at their wonderfully cozy home. If they hurried, there still would be some evening left before retiring.

They were standing in the kitchen, saying their last good-byes, when there was a rap on the door. All eyes turned toward it, wondering who was joining the festivities at such a late hour of the day. Jonathan, standing closest, moved to open it.

Perhaps Clara was popping in with the boys on their way home from Troy's family dinner. Or Dr. Luke, stopping with a cheery hello as he returned from an emergency.

But it was Jenny who stood on the back porch, shivering against the cold. Jenny with a very chilled little Mindy close at her side.

———

Virginia and Jonathan took Jenny and her child home with them. This wasn't how Virginia had intended to conclude their Christmas festivities, but after a hurried, whispered consultation they agreed it was the thing to do. Virginia noticed that Jenny carried two suitcases. At least this time she had come prepared to stay—for how long, no one asked.

Mindy was warmed with a hot bath and tucked into bed. Thumb in mouth, she curled up into a tiny ball and went to sleep almost as soon as her head touched down. Jenny was a different matter. She paced and prowled in agitated fashion until Virginia wished she could tell her to settle down. Then it dawned on her that Jenny's need for a cigarette likely had a good deal to do with it. "You may smoke in the sunroom. Just close the door to the house and open the window," she conceded. She hated the thought of smoke in the house at all. "You know, Jenny, some nourishing food would be better than a cigarette."

"Yes, Mother," she interrupted in mock submission. But Virginia could tell she was relieved to be able to have her cigarette without going out to face the cold.

"Please don't smoke in the bedroom," Virginia went on, feeling that the rules should be clearly laid out at the start. "We'll leave a light on if you need to come down in the night."

Jenny nodded mutely.

Virginia's tone softened. "If there's anything you need, please let me know. You are welcome to stay as long as you wish."

Even as she spoke the words, Virginia inwardly cringed. She had been so looking forward to having Jonathan all to herself. To finally be able to make a home for him. For the two of them. And now . . . But there was no way she would turn Jenny and her little one away. It would be not only selfish. It was totally unthinkable.

"I don't expect to be long," answered Jenny, but she gave no further hint of what was going on, what she had in mind.

It wasn't until two days later that Jenny began to talk about her situation. Hayden had left her. No—not really left her. He had kicked her out. Well, no—not really kicked her out. He had simply come home with another woman. Jenny, in a wild burst of temper, had decided to move out. Virginia could tell she was already having second thoughts.

"I shouldn't have left," she stormed on the third day. "I should have grabbed her by her fake blond hair and thrown her out. *I* should have thrown *him* out!" she finished, calling him an unrepeatable name.

Virginia made no comment.

"It's the kid," Jenny spat out on the fourth day, venom in her voice. "Hayden never wanted kids. He told me he'd kill me if I had another one."

Virginia's face showed her shock, and she stood frozen in place as if she'd been struck herself.

"He didn't mean it literally." Jenny swore. "It's just an expression, Virginia." But Jenny's explanation did not erase the horror from Virginia's heart.

On the sixth day, Jenny thumped down the stairs. "I'm going back," she announced to Virginia, who was busy washing up the breakfast dishes.

"Wait, Jenny." Virginia wiped her hands on her apron. "Are you sure? Think about it."

"I've already thought about it. I'm going back. I know I can get him back again if . . ."

Virginia waited for the rest of the sentence. It did not come.

"If what, Jenny?"

"If I dump the kid." The words were out there. Blunt and ugly.

Virginia's face paled and her heart felt like it was being squeezed. "What do you mean? I . . . I don't understand. . . ."

"There's a home for kids in the city. I've thought about it for a long time. She'd be better off there anyway."

"But you can't just . . ." Virginia was shaking, and she couldn't finish her sentence.

"She's my kid."

"That's my point. How can you just . . . just desert your own child?"

"It's not exactly desertion. It'll be best for her, too, in the long run. She might even be adopted into a family."

"But how could you, Jenny? How can you stand there

and talk about giving up your own child?"

"Don't preach at me, Virginia. I'm finished with your sermons."

"Jenny, that's not fair. I have not preached one single sermon in the time you have been with us."

"Maybe not out loud. But your eyes have preached at me every time you look at me."

"What you think you see in my eyes is your own interpretation. Not necessarily what I am thinking or feeling."

"I think I have a pretty good idea what you're thinking. I've known you a long time. I've heard your thoughts and opinions often enough. Enough to know that you must have a pretty low view of me."

"Please . . . could we talk? Please, Jenny, just sit down. I'll make some coffee and we'll talk about this."

"I'm not changing my mind. It's the only way I can work through this."

"All right," Virginia conceded. "I'm not asking you to change your mind—if you're sure. But let's just talk about it before you . . . you go through with this."

Jenny sat down. Virginia felt it was a small victory. She hurried to put on the coffeepot.

"Tell me about your Hayden," she said as she placed cups on the table and took the chair across from Jenny.

Jenny took a deep breath. "He's a physical therapist. Works at the hospital. That's where I met him."

Virginia nodded. Jenny's father had told her that.

"He's great. Really, he's lots of fun. We had a fine time. Life was . . . like a big party."

"Then Mindy came along," prompted Virginia.

"Yeah. At first I thought maybe I'd be okay. He didn't mind too much. Unless she cried when he had a hangover. Then I had to hush her up. But he got more and more sullen. Didn't like the kid around. Said she made him feel old and tied down. He wanted to be free.

"We had some fights about her, but they never amounted to much. We fought some about other things too, so I didn't pay much mind to it. Then he started getting . . . more upset. Pushy when he got angry. He threw me out of the house once."

"Was that when you came. . . ?"

"Yeah. I hopped the train. Thought at first I'd never go back, I was so mad. But I soon knew that I couldn't stay away. Hayden is . . . is like no other person I've ever met. I missed him."

"So now you're going back again?"

Jenny just nodded.

"But you're going to get . . . going to do something else with Mindy?"

Jenny nodded again.

"You are sure? Absolutely sure this is what you will do?"

Jenny said, "Yes, Virginia," in a way that boded no further questions.

Virginia stood up. "Promise me one thing: Will you wait here until I talk to Jonathan?"

"He's not going to talk me out of it either, Virginia."

"He won't try. I promise."

Jenny looked surprised but eventually nodded her head in agreement. "I want to catch that afternoon train," she cautioned Virginia.

"This won't take long. I promise. I'll be right back."

Virginia grabbed a jacket from the hook by the wall and ran to the barn where Jonathan was working with the horses. Her eyes filled with tears, whether from the cold or from the anguish, she didn't know. It did not take long to spill out the whole sorry story to her husband. He held her close and let her cry. When she had finished he said simply, softly, "We can't let her do that, can we?"

"What can we do? She's determined."

"Well, we might not be able to stop her from giving up the child—I've noticed there's not much love there—but we can stop the little one from ending up in a home."

Virginia looked up into her husband's face. "You mean. . . ?"

"We can take her—if you believe that's what we should do."

"Jonathan, are you sure?"

"She's a skitterish little mite, and that's for sure. But maybe with time and love we can work it out of her."

"You mean. . . ? Oh, Jonathan, I don't know. This is such a serious decision to make so quickly. We need time to . . . to think . . . and plan."

"Do we have time?"

"Jenny intends to take the afternoon train."

"Then all I can say, Virginia, is to follow your heart." Jonathan pulled her tight against him, and Virginia wept anew.

He held her quietly for a long time and, when her tears were spent, led her to a place in the soft hay. "I think we'd better do some praying," he said, taking her hand and helping her onto the pile. They sat together and Jonathan held her hand and prayed, asking God for wisdom and clear thinking concerning little Mindy and for some way to reach Jenny with the truth.

When he had finished, he held her again. "Do you want me to come with you to the house?"

"No. No, I'm fine. But you may need to drive Jenny to the train. She's determined to go."

He nodded. "Let me know when she's ready."

Virginia returned to the house, the burden of decision still upon her. But now somehow her heart was not as heavy. She removed the jacket and hung it on its hook, then turned to Jenny still in the chair at the table. She had helped herself to more coffee.

"I've talked to Jonathan," Virginia began. "We are . . . would be honored to keep Mindy . . . until such time as you sort things through. If you decide that you want her back, just come for her. If you decide . . . otherwise . . . she will always have a home here with us."

Jenny nodded, her face without expression. Then Virginia noticed her shoulders begin to tremble. Jenny was weeping.

CHAPTER 10

*H*ad Virginia been content to feed and clothe her only, Mindy would have been an easy child. But Virginia saw behind the soulful eyes and the somber face a desperate little person crying silently for help. The little girl had not wept at Jenny's departure. Nor had she asked for her mother—not once. Her childish stoicism frightened Virginia. Mindy just sat, silent and withdrawn, with only her thumb for comfort.

Virginia did not know what to do. The child seemed to resist physical contact, drawing away whenever Virginia so much as reached out a hand to her. Jonathan tried to help, but Mindy looked up with frightened eyes whenever he came near her. Fearing she might burst into shrieks, he would back off slowly, talking softly to the little girl.

"I don't know much about children," he acknowledged, "but she looks just like a skitterish foal to me. Look at those eyes. There's absolute panic there. I suspect this is going to take a lot of time and patience."

Virginia feared she might run out of both.

Then Jonathan came up with an idea. "Old Molly is as tame as a kitten. Why don't I take Mindy out and see how the two of them will get along."

Virginia's eyes reflected her doubt, but after a full week of very little progress with the little girl, she was willing to try almost anything.

Mindy allowed Virginia to button on her coat and draw the strings of her hood. Then Jonathan, despite stiff resistance, scooped her up in his arms, and the three of them started off through the lightly falling snow to the barn.

"We're going to see the horses," Jonathan explained softly. "Horses. Have you ever seen horses before, Mindy? They are nice. I'll let you see Molly. Molly likes little people. You can even pet her if you like."

All the way to the barn he talked to her, using the words "horses" and "Molly" over and over again. Jonathan went to the pen that housed the youngest foals first. "Might be the smaller size will be less frightening for her to start with," he whispered to Virginia.

It sounded like good logic, but the long-legged, high-energy animals scampered around, pushing and nipping in their effort to get close to Jonathan, who usually brought a treat. Mindy frantically clung to Jonathan's neck, whimpering her fear.

"Not such a good idea," he murmured and moved back from the pen.

"My, they have grown!" exclaimed Virginia. "They are almost as tall as their mamas."

Jonathan grinned, proud of his horses. Virginia could tell that it took great fortitiude for him to keep away from them for the sake of the child. His normal response to the pushing and milling foals would have been to step close and rub ears and pat necks and offer handfuls of grain. But with Mindy still quaking in his arms, he held his position.

"It's about time they had names," he said, speaking softly.

"They aren't named yet?" inquired Virginia.

"I thought that was something you might like to take on."

Virginia could not hide her smile. "Well, I guess Mindy and I are going to have to work on that."

Jonathan moved down the row of mares, who watched soberly from their stalls. "Watch that black," he cautioned Virginia. "If she's spooked, she has a tendency to kick."

Virginia gave the black's hooves wide berth.

"That little brown mare—that's Chiquita. She's gentle enough, but she's not been around kids. We'll just pass her up for now."

Virginia stopped to eye the brown mare. She was a little beauty with a proud head and wide brown eyes studying first Jonathan and his unusual armful, then Virginia. Her slightly rounded sides were sleek and silky, her black mane flowing and untangled. Her face had the smallest white star on her forehead and one front foot looked like it had been dipped gently into a can of whitewash. "She's beautiful," Virginia exclaimed.

Jonathan grinned. "She's due to drop a foal in the spring. The sire's Warrior. I can hardly wait to get a look at that one. Should be some horse."

"Which one's Warrior?" Jonathan's corrals held three stallions.

"The sorrel."

Virginia knew the sorrel. As far as she was concerned, he was the most beautiful animal she had ever seen—tall and proud and muscular, with flowing mane and tail, head held high into the wind, beautiful but frightening. His tossing head and restless hooves made her think of an untamed animal of the wilds. She was concerned each time she saw Jonathan going near his corral. But Jonathan seemed to have no fear of the animal, and to Virginia's utter amazement the horse suddenly calmed when Jonathan whistled and reached out a hand toward him. But even then he was a mass of unharnessed energy, seeming ready to explode at the least provocation. "Pegasus" would have been a more apt name, Virginia noted silently as she stared at the sorrel.

As Jonathan continued along the row of horses, they turned their heads and whinnied, wanting his attention. Hooves stomped in impatience and nostrils flared while halter ropes strained against the poles that secured them.

Virginia took her eyes from the horses and looked at small Mindy. Her eyes were wide, her small body pressed up close to Jonathan's chest. She looked absolutely terrified.

"Jonathan . . . I'm not sure this is a good idea. Look at her."

Jonathan pulled his eyes from his beloved horses and gazed into the face of the child. "She does look a little nervous," he agreed, his arms tightening around the small body. "Too bad Molly is at the far end of the barn."

It appeared he had no intention of turning back. Virginia followed meekly.

Jonathan walked more quickly toward the gentle mare. "This is Molly," he explained to the child, his voice little more than a whisper. "Molly. See." He reached out a hand and stroked the rounded rump. Molly rewarded his attention by turning to look at him with soft, dark eyes. She did not so much as flick her tail. "Would you like to touch her? She's soft. Just feel." He carefully took

Mindy's hand and reached it toward the animal, but Mindy pulled it back with surprising strength. A small whimper escaped her lips.

"Okay. We won't touch. Not today."

Jonathan continued stroking the animal, who had gone back to her feeding.

"Maybe that's enough for your first day," Jonathan whispered to Mindy, giving Molly one last pat as he turned to go.

All the way out of the barn, Virginia watched the small child in Jonathan's embrace. They certainly did not want to terrorize Mindy any further. If she really did not like the horses, it would be unwise to expose her to them.

But the next day Jonathan came in midmorning and took Mindy's coat down from the hook on the wall.

"What are you doing?" asked Virginia.

"Mindy and I are going to take a little walk out to see the horses."

"Jonathan, are you sure. . . ?"

"We'll know soon enough. If she's a little more at ease with them today, then we'll know it's okay. If she still stiffens up, we'll back off."

"I don't want her . . ."

"Neither do I, Virginia. But we've got to find a way to help her if we can."

Virginia debated whether to go along or stay in the kitchen. At length she decided that for Mindy's sake, she should be there. She reached for her coat.

"You don't need to come if you'd rather not. It's chilly out there."

"I'll come."

To Virginia's eyes, Mindy looked just as frightened as before, but Jonathan was pleased. "She's not as stiff," he noted.

She still looked stiff to Virginia as she clutched Jonathan's neck, pushing herself against his chest to be as far away from the giant animals as she could get.

But every day following, Jonathan bundled the little girl up and took her to the barn to see the horses. He had moved Molly much closer to the door so they would not need to traverse the entire range of stalls before getting to her. Each day he returned the child to the house with a bit more confidence. He was sure that sometime in the not too distant future, Mindy would actually reach out to touch a horse. Virginia secretly wondered just what that would prove, what it would accomplish. Simply touching a horse was a long way from accepting people—something Mindy certainly didn't seem to be making any progress on.

But she was less wary of Jonathan. She no longer flinched away when he came near. No longer curled in a ball in the living room chair, hiding her face against its back as he approached. He always spoke to her in the same quiet voice. Gently speaking her name.

At the end of her third week with them, Jonathan came in from his evening chores and hung his heavy coat. He blew on his hands as he crossed to give Virginia a kiss on the cheek. "Brr, it's cold out there. Where's our girl?"

"In her usual place," Virginia said as she removed a pan of fragrant biscuits from the oven.

Jonathan walked on through the kitchen and over to Mindy's chair. Virginia watched as he wordlessly reached down and scooped the small child into his arms. He crossed to the rocker by the fire and sat down with her. Then, holding her close, his chin resting lightly on her silken head, the two of them rocked. Just rocked. On and on the chair squeaked softly until Virginia called them both to the table.

From then on it was a daily ritual. Midmorning Jonathan would come in from the corrals, put Mindy into her coat, and take her for her tour of the horses. At night, when the evening chores were completed, he would scoop her up and hold her close as they rocked together. Then he added something else. Morning and evening he laid his hand on the little girl's head and prayed for her.

———

They were beginning to think they were winning her heart. Mindy no longer withdrew from contact. She even pointed to her coat on the hook when Jonathan came in to get her in the morning, and she often ran to meet him when she heard his steps on the porch. Jonathan and Virginia felt greatly encouraged.

But she still did not speak. Made no effort whatsoever to talk. It troubled them, and they quietly discussed it out of her presence.

"Do you think she's deaf?" was the natural question. But Mindy did not appear to be deaf. She did respond to noise, turning her head when her name or some sudden sound drew her interest.

"Might she be mentally slow?" was their next question. But Mindy seemed to understand everything they said to her and reacted accordingly.

"I think we should try to get her to a doctor. Find out why she isn't talking," Jonathan said one night after they had tucked her in and were discussing the events of the day.

Virginia nodded. She had already discussed Mindy with her uncle Luke. He had made some suggestions, but Mindy had passed each of the small tests with no difficulty. A thorough examination seemed like the next logical step.

But before they could make the arrangements, there was a startling incident. Virginia was dishing out Mindy's morning porridge when suddenly the girl cried, "No. I don't want it," and pushed her bowl off the table.

They looked at each other in total astonishment. They did not know whether to laugh or cry. "She spoke," said Virginia, shocked, delighted, and alarmed. Mindy had never responded this way before.

Jonathan seemed to gather his senses first. "Mindy, you must not do that again," he said in a firm but controlled voice. "Look—your porridge is splattered all over the floor. Now we will have to clean it up. If you don't want porridge, you say 'No, thank you,' and then we will talk about it."

Virginia was still in a daze when she went for the cleaning rag.

It was not the last of Mindy's tantrums. By the end of her third month living with them, she screamed her protests daily, throwing whatever she held in her hand. Kicking and flailing until Virginia was sure she would injure herself. The docile, frightened child suddenly had turned into a small monster.

Virginia and Jonathan looked at each other with what-do-we-do-now expressions. They were mystified by this abrupt change in behavior. Obviously there was a great deal of anger buried in the tiny body. Once Mindy had achieved enough security to express herself, all the rage seemed to be pouring out in quick succession. Virginia was feeling utterly spent by the end of each day. Tired, drained, and strangely unsettled, she soon realized that part of the reason was not Mindy at all. Virginia was expecting their first child.

———

Jonathan was thrilled to learn he was to become a father. Virginia was happy too, though inwardly she wondered how she would ever cope. Many hours of Jonathan's day were spent with the horses. What little time he had was often taken trying to assure one small, troubled girl that she was loved and would be protected. Mindy soon felt she had every right to Jonathan's lap whenever he sat down. If he was still standing, she would tug at his trouser leg, demanding that he come to their favorite chair. Jonathan had not found any time to work on finishing the inside of the house as planned.

If he's this busy now, Virginia thought as she watched Jonathan working a horse in the corral, *how will he ever have time to be a father to another child?*

And Virginia herself, already feeling she had heavier responsibilities than she could rightly manage, wondered how in the world she could take on more—alone. She found herself praying that Mindy would quickly work through her inner turmoil. They were going to need time and strength to deal with the new baby.

———

It seemed to Virginia that one day Jonathan was coming in with snow on his shoulders and the next he was returning with corral muck nearly to his knees. As familiar as she was with farm life, she'd had no idea of the state of corrals in the spring when thawing ground and pounding hooves combined to make a foot-deep quagmire. It didn't help when that same muck was splashed up trousers and even onto jackets. The weekly laundry task had Virginia wrinkling her nose in disgust and scrubbing her hands for long minutes after with strong lye soap. She hoped the warming sun would quickly dry up the corral mud.

Now Mindy decided she should be able to go with Jonathan each time he walked out the door. Virginia had to endure an exhausting tantrum each time the door closed firmly behind him. "I don't want to wait," the child screamed over and over. "I want to go now."

Then Mindy discovered the magic word. "Please." As far as the child was concerned, "please" was to be the unlocker of all doors, the overcomer of all obstacles. One morning in the midst of Mindy's screaming to go along with Jonathan, she suddenly stopped and looked at Virginia with large, tear-filled eyes. Tipping her head slightly to one side and choking back her sobs, she implored in heart-wrenching fashion, "Please. Please I go now." It nearly broke Virginia's tender heart. She pulled the child into her arms and held her.

The little girl seemed to feel that she had won the victory.

"I'm sorry," murmured Virginia, stroking her hair, "Mindy can't go now. Later. Later you can go see Molly. But not now. No."

Mindy pulled back, her eyes dripping more tears, her mouth trembling in disappointment.

"I say please," she said, shaking her head in defiance. "When Mindy say please you are 'posed to say yes."

Virginia knew she was in for another angry outburst. How could one get a child to understand?

———

"I think we need to do some talking about names around here," Jonathan said one evening as he and Mindy sat and rocked and Virginia's knitting needles shaped a small bootee. At first Virginia thought that he was referring to the horses. She had named three of the foals, but two remained unnamed. She just hadn't been able to come up with names that suited them. Or maybe he was talking about possible names for their baby.

But then he said, "We've sort of avoided figuring out

names, but it looks to me like she might be around for a while. We'd best come up with something for her to call us."

He was not talking horses—or babies. He was talking of Mindy.

Virginia had felt awkward about it too. She nodded.

"What would you suggest?"

"Well, it seems a mite formal to ask her to call us Mr. and Mrs. Lewis."

Virginia smiled.

"And I don't think it'd be right to let her call us Jonathan and Virginia either—even if her tongue could handle it."

"Some folks use Uncle and Auntie," Virginia offered.

Jonathan nodded. Virginia saw his arms tighten slightly. "Might do," he responded.

"But you don't favor it?"

He waited before answering. "I dunno."

Not a word had come from Jenny since her departure five months earlier. It seemed that she had no intention of coming back for her child. Virginia wondered if she had found happiness with her self-centered, arrogant Hayden. She deliberately forced her thoughts back to Jonathan's words. Thinking about Jenny and her selfish husband just made her angry.

Virginia waited.

"It's just . . . well, it just seems like the little tyke needs everything we can give, and if calling us like we were her own folks would help that any . . ."

"You'd have her call us Mama and Papa?"

He nodded. "Would you object?"

Virginia thought about it. "No. No, I guess not. Seems like that's what we may end up being."

Jonathan nodded again. It seemed to be settled. He snuggled Mindy in closer against his chest.

It wasn't until the day's work was finally over, Mindy was tucked in for the night, and they had retired to their own bed that they had time to really talk. Virginia found herself looking forward each day to those precious minutes of sharing thoughts and activities and dreams for the future. It seemed to be the only time they really had alone. A time to be husband and wife. A time to catch up on not just the happenings of the day, but also the other's feelings concerning those events. It was a time to pray together. To bind their hearts and spirits. Their own private, personal time to work toward becoming truly one. It wasn't a whole lot different than when they were living with Grandmother Withers, but at least they didn't wonder if they were being overheard.

CHAPTER 11

*J*onathan had secured the help of a woman in town to care for Grandmother Withers. Mrs. Cadbury came by three times a week and made sure that the fires were burning, that the shopping was done, that the needs of Grandmother were met. But with the coming of spring, Virginia knew that Mrs. Cadbury, no matter how willing she might be, would not be able to also care for the large flower garden. One noon over lunch she broached the subject with Jonathan.

"I'm sure Grandmother's flower beds are in sore need of attention. They've been left far too long already."

He nodded. "I've been thinking on it. I did hire a boy to do the main weeding, but I'm sure he doesn't know much about plants."

Virginia, relieved to know that the main weeding had been done, said, "I was wondering if I should go in for a day or two."

Jonathan looked at Virginia, a frown creasing his brow.

"I won't overdo it. Just trim things up a bit and maybe put in a few stakes."

"If you get to feeling tired, you'll stop?"

Virginia nodded.

The next morning when she had finished the breakfast dishes and placed a lunch in the icebox for Jonathan, Virginia hurried Mindy out the door. "We're going to see Grandmother," she said to the upturned little face.

"Which grandma?" asked Mindy, having already been introduced to three of them over the months she had been with Virginia and Jonathan.

"Grandmother Withers."

"Oh." That was all. As though everything was now in proper perspective.

"I'm going to work in her garden, and you are going to be a good girl."

"Can I help, Mama?"

"We'll see," Virginia responded, her heart twisting with bittersweet emotions at the seldom-used "Mama."

Grandmother Withers was already in the yard, trowel in hand and a broad smile on her face as she watched them arrive. Virginia could see that she had a crink in her back when she tried to straighten up. She reached a hand around to support her spine. Virginia noted the brief shadow in her eyes from pain she was unable to fully hide.

They started to work in the yard together, Grandmother Withers chatting and pointing and giving instructions, Virginia doing her best to carry them out. Mindy followed them around with a small trowel in her hand, digging up dirt here and there and mostly getting in the way. Virginia was pleased to see that the boy hired by Jonathan had been doing his job. The beds were remarkably weed free.

She returned home that night extremely weary but

happy with what had been accomplished.

"I don't know whose son you selected for weeding," she informed Jonathan, "but he has been doing a first-rate job on your grandmother's garden. If I go in every other week or so, we should manage just fine."

It was a big relief to Virginia. She had been fretting about Grandmother's yard work. And her own days were not getting easier. Even though the corrals had dried out so there wasn't as much heavy laundry, her back still ached after every day spent washing clothes, sweeping floors, and caring for Mindy.

In fact, her back seemed to ache a lot. It was all she could do to keep up with the weeds in her own vegetable and flower gardens. She showed Mindy how to feed the chickens, and the three-year-old took great delight in filling the watering and feeding dishes. Mindy also begged to be the one to feed the dog and the two barn cats Jonathan had decided the farm needed. In fact, Mindy seemed to take more pleasure from the animals than she did from humans. Virginia heard her steady chatter as she placed the food dishes. Virginia continually marveled at the child's vocabulary. Once she had decided to talk, all the words seemed to be in place.

But there were still the temper tantrums. The wet beds. The continually wizened thumb from all the sucking. Virginia feared that the child's teeth would be damaged. But she didn't want to resort yet to pepper or vanilla extract. The child needed assurance—and discipline. But carefully measured out, the one balanced with the other.

———

Sundays were the only days that the farm routine changed. Other than feeding, Jonathan did not work the horses on Sunday. The Lewises slept in a bit later on Sunday morning. At least they attempted it. Mindy usually wakened them earlier than they would have wished. Almost before the sun peeked over the horizon, the door was flung open and Mindy bounced onto their bed.

"I think it's up time. My tummy's hungry" was her usual wake-up call.

Virginia was tempted to hide her head under the pillow.

More often than not, Jonathan sent Mindy on back to her room to get dressed, and he crawled out to pull on shirt and trousers. "You sleep," he'd tell Virginia with a kiss, "I'll find her something that will hold her until breakfast." And Virginia often did go back to sleep. She knew Jonathan would call her in plenty of time to get them all ready for church.

What Jonathan and Mindy found to do on those early Sunday mornings Virginia was not sure. She only knew that the house was nice and quiet. She sometimes heard the distant barking of the dog or the welcoming whinny of a horse. By the time she had talked herself into getting up, the fire had been built, the chickens and farm pets fed, and their one cow milked. All things looked to be in order, and Mindy seemed to have either forgotten or else had something put into her hungry tummy.

One thing is for sure, Virginia told herself as she watched the little girl dig into her breakfast. *Her appetite has certainly improved.*

Along with the appetite gradually had come a more wholesome, healthy appearance. She was still tiny for her age—Virginia supposed she always would be—but she now did not look so pale and thin.

Virginia's one regret concerning Sunday was that, try as they might, they had not been able to help Mindy get over her shyness with the grandparents. They coaxed and cajoled and even tried gentle bribes, but the little one could not be persuaded to let go of Jonathan's hand. Belinda baked fancy cookies, Drew offered sticks of fresh spearmint, and Jenny's father, Mindy's actual grandfather, came to church with pockets laden with treasures for her. It was especially difficult for him when Mindy clung to Jonathan or buried her face in Virginia's skirts. She had discovered her own small, safe world, and she seemed still doubtful and hesitant to extend its borders or let anyone else in—even her own grandpa.

Virginia watched Mr. Woods' disappointment with keen understanding. He had already lost his daughter; now he was unable to make friends with his grandchild. Virginia repeatedly tried to reassure him, "She just needs time. It took us several months to win her over." She could have added that they still had many days when they doubted that they had indeed won her over. Though certainly they had come a long way. Not only did Mindy love Jonathan, she loved his horses. Especially Molly. She was never happier than when Jonathan would boost her up onto Molly's back and lead her around the yard, or place her up in front of him in the saddle as he rode Cricket or Chiquita off to check a pasture fence or see how the grass was holding out or if the stream was clear of debris.

Mindy would return, cheeks aglow, hair windswept, and a shine to her eyes that made Virginia smile.

———

The months of late summer and early fall seemed unusually hot to Virginia, who was feeling the weight of the child she carried. The baby was not due to be born until early January, and at times Virginia wondered how she ever would make it through the months ahead. She had escaped the ordeal of morning sickness, for which she was grateful, but she did seem to have unusual pain in her legs and back. Perhaps it was the lifting about of young Mindy or the work in the gardens, she told herself. She tried to keep her complaints to herself, not wanting to concern Jonathan.

But he seemed to read the tiredness in her eyes and often expressed his concern. He made sure she did not need to carry wood or water, and he went to town to order one of those new washing machines so she wouldn't need to stand over a scrub board. Virginia was concerned that the machine might be an extravagance they could not afford, but Jonathan pointed to the young horses in the nearby pasture. "They will help pay for it someday. They're looking better all the time."

But Virginia knew it would be some time until Jonathan put any of the animals up for sale. He didn't want all his hard work and careful schooling spoiled in a matter of days by someone unskilled in horse handling.

———

Indian summer allowed Virginia to get extra garden vegetables canned and put the rest in the root cellar. She was also able to clean up all her flower beds and mulch her roses. Jonathan was particularly pleased with the unseasonably warm weather. Each additional day of sunshine meant saving on the hay for the horses during the long winter ahead.

Mindy continued to thrive—at least physically. Virginia sometimes wondered if they ever would be able to take the anger out of the youngster. Her sudden bursts of rage caught them off guard on many occasions. They were never sure just what might bring about a tantrum—often something as simple as Jonathan leaving without her, a tangled shoelace, a book that wouldn't stay open at the right page, a kitten that didn't want to be carried.

Virginia wished she'd had more time—and more information—from Jenny. There was so much about the child she didn't know. She did not even know her birth date, and Mr. Woods himself was only able to give her a vague idea. They picked a date and marked it on the calendar. Until they knew better, that would be the day they would celebrate the child's birthday.

In the first weeks and months, Virginia had hoped Jenny would return. It seemed only right and fair that the little one be raised by her own mother. But as time moved toward their first year together, Virginia began to fear the possibility. She didn't know how she could bear it if Jenny suddenly appeared on their doorstep and announced that she had come for her daughter. She didn't know how Jonathan would manage the loss either.

And how would Mindy react? Would she remember her mother at all? If she did, would she embrace her or cower in a corner with her thumb? Virginia wasn't sure.

She now called them Mama and Papa as naturally as if she had been born into the home. Though she was quite at ease with either one of them, it was Jonathan whom she adored. Papa was the first name she called every morning, the last good-night of the evening. Papa was the one she mimicked, the one she squealed over with delight. So it hadn't really been the horses that had won the little girl, Virginia realized, but the man who daily carried her off to the barn to meet the horses. Because he loved them, Mindy learned to love them too. Because she had learned to trust the strength of his arms, she learned to relax in them. To lean against the broadness of his chest, knowing that she was safe and loved.

———

The first snow came in big, fluffy flakes, causing

Mindy's large eyes to widen further. "Look, Mama," she called to Virginia. "Chicken feathers."

Virginia laughed and went to join the child at the kitchen window.

"No, it's not chicken feathers. It's called snow. Don't you remember it from last year? It falls and falls from the sky until all of the ground and the house and the barns are covered."

"And the kitties?"

"No. Not the kitties. The kitties will stay in the barn."

"And Murphy?"

"No. Murphy will go in his doghouse."

Mindy's eyes grew big with concern. "Papa?"

"No. Not Papa. Papa will come to the house with us."

The child looked relieved. But she still seemed a bit doubtful. "When will he come?" she fretted as she watched the big flakes continue to fall.

Virginia moved from the window and looked at the kitchen clock. "Not for a while yet. He has lots of chores to do."

Mindy stood at the window, eyes straining to see into the storm. "He'd better come quick," she said after many minutes. "He might get stuck."

"He won't get stuck."

"He might. It's getting deep. Over my boots."

"It's not over Papa's boots. He's tall."

Mindy considered that, seeming less concerned. But she would not leave her post at the window. Virginia continued the supper preparations. She did not need to guess when Jonathan was on his way in. A squeal from the window told her that Mindy had spotted him through the flurries of snow.

———

"I think maybe I'll see if I can find you a tree tomorrow," Jonathan told Virginia just as they were retiring for the night. Virginia found it hard to believe that another Christmas was approaching, but the calendar on the wall, the huge drifts of snow against the porch rails, and the weight of the baby she was carrying all confirmed the fact that the year was drawing to a close.

"That would be good," she murmured from her side of the bed.

"Thought I might take the Scamp with me if it's not too cold."

Jonathan had taken to referring to Mindy as "the Scamp" when they were alone. Hearing the love in his voice when he used the term, Virginia only smiled. "She'd like that."

"I'll set the tree in the entry and let it thaw some. We can put it up tomorrow night."

"I'll get the decorations ready."

The next day held a sharp chill, but no wind was blowing so they deemed the day fit for Mindy to venture forth.

Full of anticipation, her mittened hand held firmly in Jonathan's, she announced, "We're gonna get a Christmas tree." But Virginia wondered if she remembered just what a Christmas tree was all about. There was so much of Mindy's short childhood that she seemed to have blocked out.

"Papa's gonna pull me on the sled."

"That will be fun."

"If he gets tired, I'll pull him."

Jonathan laughed.

And off they went, Jonathan tugging the rope that sent the sled through the drifts, spraying Mindy with light, cold fluff. Virginia could hear her squeal even through the panes of glass that kept the cold at bay.

They will have fun, she mused as she watched. *I wish I could have joined them.* She looked down, placing a hand lovingly on her protruding abdomen. *But I'm not sure it would have been wise for you and me to tramp through the drifts just now. I sometimes get the impression that you are getting a little anxious to join this family.*

CHAPTER 12

$\mathcal{M}$indy was thrilled over everything that had to do with Christmas. For the next several days after her trip with Jonathan into the woods for the tree, she coaxed and pleaded with him to go for another. She was not satisfied when Jonathan and Virginia tried to explain that only one Christmas tree in their living room was necessary. "We need to save the others so we'll have them in years to come," Jonathan told the little girl. She insisted that there were lots and lots of trees in the woods. Virginia said that they had room for only one tree, to which she replied that another one could go in "that corner."

"But we have enough decorations for just one tree," went on Virginia patiently.

"They could share" was her reply.

Mindy finally had her attention diverted from Christmas trees when Virginia began to bake cookies. Mindy, who loved to get her hands in cookie dough, begged to help. Virginia placed a chair up to the table and gave the child a handful of dough and a small wooden dowel for a rolling pin. She rolled, then scrunched the dough into a misshapen ball, then rolled some more. The dough got smaller and smaller as little nibbles were taken and small bits fell to the kitchen floor. By the time Virginia finished her own task and turned to see if Mindy's cookies were ready for the pan, there was very little left. When Virginia asked what had happened, though she already had a pretty good idea, Mindy answered that Murphy must have gotten it.

Virginia followed up with a little lecture about telling the truth at all times. Mindy simply cocked her head to one side, pointed down at the mess on the floor beneath her chair, and said, "Well, if I opened the door up for Murphy, he would get it."

But the thing that seemed to intrigue Mindy the most was the Nativity scene. Small wooden figures on the fireplace hearth represented various parts of the Christmas story. Over and over she asked for the story about the baby Jesus. Over and over either Virginia or Jonathan had to act out the swoop of the angels over the night sky, the startled shepherds jumping up from their blankets and then rushing off to Bethlehem to see the tiny miracle in the manger. Over and over the camels had to thump their way across the sand desert of the hearth, looking for the baby Jesus. Each time, the little girl would clap her hands and squeal, then point to the manger where he lay. "Here he is. Here he is. Right here." And the Magi would find the baby.

She never tired of the story, of moving the pieces about, or the playacting. When she saw the children of the Sunday school act out the scene in the Christmas program, her eyes filled with excitement. And when the wise men arrived looking for the Christ child, she stood up in the pew and squealed aloud, "There he is. Right there," to everyone's delight.

———————

Virginia had hoped to have the family Christmas at her house, but with the baby's coming so near-at-hand her mother talked her out of it. "There will be lots of Christmases," Belinda told her. "There is no use pushing yourself for this one. What with Mindy, the baby on the way and all, I think you already have your hands full."

Virginia did not argue for long. It was agreed they would all go to Clara's. Belinda insisted that she would go over early and help Clara with the dinner, that Virginia would "only be in the way." The two laughed and looked at each other with womanly understanding.

With those arrangements in place, Virginia was able to enjoy a leisurely Christmas morning.

Jonathan had done most of the shopping for Mindy's Christmas stocking. Virginia did not feel up to struggling down the aisles of the local hardware store trying to pick out a dolly and a skipping rope. She was pleased with Jonathan's purchases and could hardly wait for Christmas morning to see the eyes of the small child light up.

It was even more fun than she had imagined. Mindy stared for a long time, openmouthed, unable or unwilling to move from the spot.

"Go ahead," coaxed Jonathan. "It's your stocking. Your Christmas stocking. Go see what's in there." Mindy stood stock-still.

"Come. Papa will go with you."

He took her by the hand and led her to where the red-striped stocking hung.

"There, lift it down." But Jonathan had to do it for her.

"Now, come over here and we'll look and see what's in it." He took her hand and led her back to their chair.

Together they extracted each item, Mindy's eyes growing wider and her face full of wonder. She exclaimed over everything that came from the stocking, clapping or squealing, hands over her mouth.

When the last item was laid on Jonathan's lap, she looked over at Virginia. "Did you see it? Did you see it, Mama? It's all for me." She waved two little arms in a large arc.

Then she looked up at Jonathan. "I think I should share with Mama," she said solemnly. And she picked up the baby doll wrapped in the blanket that Virginia had crocheted and took it over to Virginia. "There," she exclaimed, seeming to feel much better. "Now you have a baby."

Before Virginia could respond, Jonathan moved from his chair to the floor, picked up the child, and sat her on his knee. "Mama doesn't need your baby," he said, eyes warm with anticipation. "Very soon now Mama is going to get a baby of her own. It's going to be tiny—about so big. But it won't be a dolly like your baby. It will be a real baby like Aunt Clara's. Only this one will be much smaller—and ours."

Mindy listened. "Mine too?"

"Yours too."

"Can I hold it?"

"When we help you. You and I will rock it in the big chair while Mama gets our supper."

"Will it cry?"

"Sometimes."

"I hope not much. It hurts my ears when baby Martin cries, and it makes my tummy jitter."

"We'll try to keep it happy so it won't cry too much."

Mindy looked at Jonathan, large eyes solemn. She

shrugged. "I guess it's okay," and she hopped up to go and retrieve her doll baby. But before she lifted the bundle from Virginia's lap, she asked seriously, "Do you want to keep this one till you get yours?"

"Thank you," said Virginia blinking joyful tears from her eyes. "I can wait. You can have your dolly."

———

Virginia felt strange throughout that final day of December. By midafternoon she knew that she was feeling more than an upset stomach. Soon she was counting contractions, trying hard not to feel alarm as she waited for Jonathan to come in from the barn. At last she decided she dared not wait longer.

"Mindy, do you think you can find Papa?"

Mindy's eyes glowed as she nodded her head.

"Now, listen carefully," said Virginia, kneeling before the small girl. "Mama does not want you to go alone into the barn. Do you understand? I just want you to look around the corrals and see if Papa is there. If he isn't, then go to the barn door and call. Just holler for him. If he is there, he will hear you. You wait—right there by the door."

Mindy looked puzzled. "Why can't I go in the barn?"

"Because. Because of the horses. They might . . . might not see it's you and . . . think you are Murphy or something . . . and get nervous."

Virginia thought of the nervous black mare. She was on the verge of changing her mind about letting the little girl go when another contraction seized her, this one stronger and longer than the others.

She waited for it to pass, her breath coming in little gasps. "Mama, are you sick?" asked Mindy anxiously.

Virginia took a deep breath and managed a wobbly

smile. "Mama's okay. I just need Papa. You see if you can find him and ask him to come to the house."

She quickly put Mindy's coat on her as she spoke and prayed that she would not have another contraction until the child was out the door.

She watched from the kitchen window as the little girl made her way through the snow to the corrals. It appeared that Jonathan was not there. Virginia saw Mindy look around and then head for the barn.

Another contraction took her, and she had to ease herself down onto a kitchen chair, supporting herself against the table. *Calm yourself. Calm yourself*, she kept repeating. *Breathe deeply. Another breath.*

At last the pain eased off, and Virginia, face flushed, decided that she'd best make it to her bed before the next one hit.

She managed the stairs, stripped the bed of the blankets in one large sweep, and got the flannels from the closet where she had them stored. She had just managed to arrange them when she heard the door bang and Jonathan calling her name. *Mindy found him.* Virginia breathed a prayer of thanks and lowered herself to the bed just as another contraction tightened her abdomen. She could not even answer Jonathan's call. She heard his footsteps on the stairs and, sure he had not stopped to remove his barn boots, had the silly thought that he likely was leaving tracks on her clean floors.

"Are you okay?" was his anxious question as he burst through the door, Mindy in one arm. His eyes moved quickly about the bedroom. Blankets scattered across the floor. White flannels haphazardly spread across the bed. Virginia crouched on the edge, her face pale, her hands on her stomach.

"I think so."

"I've got to get Luke."

"Get Mama."

"Mama. Okay." But he seemed dazed. He moved Mindy to his other arm.

"Will the motorcar start?" asked Virginia.

"I've been keeping a heater going in the car shed."

Virginia was unaware that he had planned that far ahead.

"What shall I do with Mindy?" he asked anxiously.

"You'd best take her with you."

"Then you'll be all alone."

Virginia managed a chuckle. "And what good do you think she'd do if she were here?"

"Well, she found me."

"Yes," admitted Virginia with a nod of her head. "But I don't think she has much experience delivering babies."

Jonathan nodded. "I'll hurry," he promised and turned to go. Just before he passed through the door, he turned back one last time, his face ashen. "Don't . . . do anything until I get back." And then he was gone, leaving Virginia still chuckling until another contraction robbed her of mirth.

———

The baby, a girl, arrived twelve minutes before midnight. Though she was tiny, she appeared healthy, with a cry loud enough to hurt anyone's ears and make tummies jitter.

Mindy, who had been put to bed, tiptoed from her room, rubbing sleepy eyes, and Jonathan picked her up and gave her one small peek at the newcomer before tucking her back in her bed.

Dr. Luke and Belinda both were on hand for the delivery. Virginia felt exhausted when it was finally over and was more than content to swallow the sleeping preparation that Luke held out to her. She knew her baby would be in good hands.

"Let me have one more look at her," she implored as she lay back against her pillows, and the baby was placed in her arms once more.

"She's beautiful, isn't she? Isn't she, Jonathan?" The proud father agreed, reaching out to touch one tiny curled fist.

"Have you named her?" asked Belinda.

Virginia's eyes moved to meet Jonathan's. "We've picked two names. Now we need to decide which one it'll be. What do you think? Is she a Martha Joy or a Sarah Ann?"

Jonathan dipped his head. "I'm leaning toward Martha."

Virginia looked down at her baby. "I think you're right. I think she's a Martha."

"Maybe the next one will be a Sarah."

Virginia's eyes flashed upward to meet her husband's. "Don't you dare say a thing like that to me. Not until at least . . . tomorrow morning."

He bent over to kiss her, chuckling. Then he gently lifted his daughter, kissed Virginia again, and whispered, "Get some sleep, Mama. You've had a big day."

———

In the morning, as usual, Mindy bounced into the bedroom. Jonathan was quick to rise from the bed, his finger to his lips. "Shh. Mama's sleeping."

But Virginia already had heard her. "Is it morning already?" she asked sleepily, stirring slowly to look around.

"Not just morning—a new year."

Virginia smiled. "Does Grandma Marty know yet? And Grandmother Withers? And Clara?"

"Not yet. We didn't think we should rouse them at midnight. But they'll know soon enough. Mindy and I are going to get in the car and go spread the news."

"Where's our baby—baby Martha?" Virginia said, savoring the name on her tongue.

"She's with her grandmother, getting rocked. She'll likely be thoroughly spoiled before I even get a chance."

"Mama's still here?"

"She said she'll stay until you're on your feet again."

"Uncle Luke?"

"He went home last night—or this morning, however you want to think of it. Why don't you try to get some more sleep?"

Virginia rolled over onto her side. "I think I will," and she closed her eyes.

CHAPTER 13

The days of lying abed after childbirth, while the sounds of an active family drifted up the stairway, were difficult for Virginia. She longed to be downstairs, a part of the household activity. And though her mother brought baby Martha to see her often, Virginia wanted the opportunity to care for her own child.

There were lots of visitors. The great-grandparents arrived—as well as aunts and uncles, cousins and extended family members, and friends—and Virginia disliked being propped up in bed to receive them rather than down serving tea. But it was such fun to show off the baby.

Virginia was thankful when she was finally allowed out of bed and down to the living room. It felt good to be moving about again. Good to be a part of the family life. She chatted with her mother, read to Mindy, and took over Martha's bath time. She made sure the coffeepot was on for Jonathan when he came in midmorning, and fixed him hot chocolate at the end of the day. It was like their old routine, except that her mother occupied the upstairs guest room and a very small new family member slept in the cradle beside their own bed or wailed to be fed or changed. Virginia had never felt happier.

————

Virginia was both pleased and sad when the day came that she was able to be on her own. She was happy to be able to run her own home again, but she had enjoyed having her mother with her. "Baby Martha will miss you, Mama," she said as she hugged Belinda.

"Oh, she will see me often. You'll likely weary of me popping in."

"Never. Come as often as you like."

Belinda turned to tell Mindy good-bye. The little girl still did not allow hugs and seldom would even speak to anyone other than Virginia and Jonathan. Now she pointed at the cradle. "Don't forget her."

Belinda laughed. "Oh, I'm not taking your baby. She stays here with you. That's Mindy's baby sister."

"You take her," said Mindy solemnly. "I don't like her much."

————

They had laughed about Mindy's comment, but a few days later Virginia noted a change in the little girl. She sat quietly in the big rocker where she and Jonathan rocked so frequently, eyes half-closed and thumb in mouth. Virginia had not seen her suck her thumb for a long time except at bedtime.

When Jonathan came in from his hours of outside work, Mindy bounced down off the chair and ran to meet him. "Let's rock," she said, tugging on his arm before he could even remove his jacket. "Whoa," Jonathan responded. "Let me warm my fingers first."

But Mindy was impatient as Jonathan held his hands over the cookstove, rubbing them together to take away winter's chill.

Jonathan moved to Martha's cradle. The baby was awake, silently contemplating her limited world. When Jonathan spoke to her, she turned her head toward the sound. He grinned. "Now, aren't you one bright little filly. You already know your papa's voice."

Virginia, from her spot on the sofa, smiled. Was it the voice or just the sound? Well, perhaps Jonathan was right. Maybe the child did recognize the familiar.

"Well, now, let's just get you out of there for a little talk, shall we," Jonathan enthused, lifting out the wee one. Martha responded by making faces, and he made faces back at her. He tucked the tiny baby into one arm and reached with the other toward Mindy.

"Now let's go rock, Mindy."

But Mindy had changed her mind. She stood apart, mute and big-eyed, her thumb firmly fixed in her mouth. She did not say a word. Did not even shake her head. Then the big eyes closed, blocking out the world.

"Mindy, come sit with Mama," Virginia, who had been carefully watching, invited her. But there was no indication that the little girl even heard her words.

"We'll read your new Christmas book," coaxed Virginia further, a promise that usually brought the little girl at a run. Still no response.

Jonathan and Virginia exchanged silent messages.

"Here," murmured Jonathan, passing the baby off to Virginia. "Hold her until we settle into the chair, then bring her to me."

He went to Mindy and lifted her up into his arms and

held her close, his head against her hair, for what seemed to Virginia to be a long time. Nothing was said. They just stood there, the little girl held firmly and lovingly against her papa. When he finally moved, he went to their chair and sat down; Mindy still held tightly. For a few silent moments they rocked gently back and forth; then Jonathan looked over at Virginia and gave a nod.

"Let's you and me rock our baby for a little while," Jonathan said. Mindy squirmed. "There's lots of room on Papa's lap, and baby Martha wants to rock too."

Virginia leaned over and placed Martha on Jonathan's free arm.

For a time Mindy seemed frozen in position. Her thumb returned to her mouth. After a few moments she withdrew it long enough to say, "It's too crowded. She's pushing me. Give her back to Mama."

Jonathan was firm. "Papa wants to hold her. I haven't seen her all day. She was sleeping when I went out this morning."

"She should sleep some more. Put her over there." Mindy's small head nodded toward the cradle.

"She wants to be awake for a little while, see her family. Don't you, Martha? See—she's looking right at you."

Mindy scrunched her eyes tightly.

"She likes to rock with her papa and her big sister," went on Jonathan. "Did you know she can hold on to fingers? Look. Look how she holds Papa's."

But Mindy would not look.

Virginia watched, realizing that Mindy obviously was feeling a good deal of insecurity and jealousy over the new baby. They had just begun to think that Mindy had made adjustments. Her temper tantrums were not as often nor as fierce. Now were they to revert back to the old behavior? She hoped with all her heart that they were not. The days of Mindy's flare-ups had been difficult for all of them.

Even as Virginia watched, Mindy slid down off Jonathan's lap and walked silently away.

"Are you going for your book?" asked Jonathan. Mindy made no response.

"If you bring it, Papa will read to you and you can turn the pages."

Still no indication that Mindy had heard his words.

"I think Martha would like to hear the story too."

Mindy climbed the steps, not even turning her head.

"Oh dear," said Virginia when she was sure the little girl was out of earshot. "I think we have a bad case of nose-out-of-joint here. What do we do now?"

Jonathan hoisted Martha up and kissed her on the top of her little head.

"Hopefully this won't last long," he said with a sigh. "I thought she was coming along well."

"I think she was. I hope we don't have to go through the whole painful process all over again."

Jonathan just shook his head and sighed.

"Do you think you should just sort of . . . not fuss over Martha?" Virginia gently questioned.

"Ignore my own baby?"

"Well, not really ignore her. Just not make it obvious. Not when Mindy is around."

"You have to start early. Let them know your voice and your touch. Feel comfortable and safe around you." Virginia knew that Jonathan was thinking of his foals even though he was speaking about the child he held in his arms. She opened her mouth to object, then quickly closed it again. Perhaps the same methods did work for children.

Jonathan continued, "I fear that's what Mindy missed. I'm not about to let that happen with Martha.

151

Mindy has to learn. To know that this child is loved too. I'm not sure what's the best way. Far as I know, if I just try to let her know that she is still loved even though baby Martha is too, eventually she will not feel so abandoned or uncertain."

Virginia frowned. It was tricky, hitting this balance. "Mindy has already suffered so much. I hate to put her through any more," she said quietly. "Baby Martha is held and handled and loved. She wouldn't even notice."

"I would."

It was true—Jonathan had a right to cuddle his child. To bond with her early. To know the excitement when he first saw her recognize his voice. Virginia would not, could not, deny him that.

"We'll work with Mindy as gently, as lovingly, as we can," went on Jonathan, "but we cannot let her take over our family."

Virginia nodded, but there was still concern in her heart. How were they going to manage Mindy? And baby Martha?

―――――

Mindy continued to be totally unpredictable. One day she would be silent and withdrawn, the next she would wake up crying and continue through most of the day. At times she threw such ugly temper tantrums that Virginia was exhausted dealing with them. Mindy sometimes nearly bowled Jonathan over when he came in the door; at other times she would not even go near him when he called to her.

She seemed to lose all interest in the farm animals. She did not wish to feed the chickens, play with the kittens, or tussle with Murphy. Virginia found it much easier to do the tasks herself than to coax and fight with the young girl.

And Mindy started to wet her bed again. Virginia did not need the additional laundry in the dead of winter with the baby's washing already keeping her busy.

Virginia did not dare leave the two little ones unattended, even for a few minutes. With Mindy's obvious dislike of the baby, Virginia feared she might dump her from the cradle or cause some other harm. By each day's end Virginia felt worn out and discouraged. She did hope and pray that Mindy's difficult behavior would end quickly.

Jonathan could be of little help during the day, other than to support and encourage her. He was working full time with the five two-year-old mares who were to be the future of the farm. He planned to have them ready for early spring sale.

"I'd love to keep that young filly you named Cinnamon," he told Virginia one day. "She shows real promise."

"Then why don't you?"

"We need the money. She should bring the best price of any of them."

Virginia had dubbed the three fillies Nutmeg, Ginger, and Cinnamon, much to Jonathan's amusement. But he had let the names stand. "So what are you going to call the two colts? Mustard and Horseradish?" he had quipped.

Virginia decided to pretend she had missed the jest. "The color's all wrong for Mustard. Otherwise . . . I like it. Though I don't care that much for Horseradish. But Ginger, Nutmeg, and Cinnamon—the colors are right. Just look at them."

Jonathan had nodded and grinned, rolling his eyes.

The two young colts ended up being Navajo and Cherokee. Jonathan had smiled his agreement. "They have the pride and strength of young braves. I like that."

But now the five were being prepared to fetch a good

price at the local market. Someone else would be given the pleasure of showing off the fine animals.

Virginia, too, had been drawn to Cinnamon. Besides being a beauty, she was the most responsive to affection, seeming to thrive on neck pats and nose rubs. She was always the first to the corral fence whenever Virginia ventured outside, which was a very rare treat on the wintry days following the birth of Martha. But Cinnamon called to her each time that she so much as appeared on the porch steps. Virginia wished she could have spent more time with the filly.

Even young Mindy, on her trips out with Jonathan, had the horse gently nudging for more attention, though Mindy now usually shook off or ignored such attempts. In the past she would have climbed the corral fence and never seemed to tire of patting one shiny neck or another.

Virginia wished they did not have to sell any of their animals. She had grown attached to them and knew that Jonathan had as well. But it was true—they needed the money. The animals were not meant to be pets but were to make a living for the Lewis household.

We need the money, Virginia reminded herself again. It had been tough getting started. What with the expense of building a house, taking on the raising of a child, and having a new baby. She was almost surprised and very thankful that they had not had to extend their debt. Only the house was not completely paid for. Jonathan had thought he might have to spend money on extra winter feed, but the mild winter had thus far helped them in that regard.

Still, it was a worry, this effort to balance accounts. It weighed on Virginia, and though Jonathan did not speak of it much, she knew that it weighed on him as well.

We'll make it, she kept telling herself. *God is faithful, and before we know it, spring will be here again.* She had every confidence that Jonathan would get a good price for his fine animals.

Virginia would have scarcely noted the slow passing of winter had not little Martha continued to fill out her newborn garments. Then Virginia was reminded to glance at the calendar on the wall. Martha was already two months old. In spite of the fullness of her days and the many tasks required in caring for family, Virginia knew that "baby days" passed quickly.

Now if only they could just guide Mindy through her current emotional turmoil with some measure of success. Virginia felt it would make life so much easier.

———

Cinnamon had developed a limp, and Jonathan was puzzled as to why. As carefully as he examined her hoof and leg, he could not find anything that seemed to be wrong. He drove into town and consulted Danny by phone, who was in his last year of veterinary studies. Danny suggested everything he knew, but nothing seemed to help the filly.

Virginia fretted and stewed, then prayed, felt peace, then fretted some more. There was a house payment coming due at the bank, and the money would be needed. And they would need funds in reserve. It would be a long time before another string of horses was ready for market. Last year's foals were just in the early stage of training and development. To sell them now would mean a big reduction in price and would jeopardize future profits.

Jonathan worked daily with young Cinnamon, massaging, heating, icing, rubbing—he did everything he could think of, and all to no avail.

"Can't you just sell her as she is?" asked Virginia anxiously.

"No one wants a horse that isn't sound."

"Will she need to be put down?" Virginia finally expressed her deepest fear.

"No. Certainly not as she is now. She's mobile enough. Doesn't seem to be in a lot of pain. She just wouldn't do for riding or driving."

"Maybe she's faking it," suggested Virginia.

"Faking it?" Jonathan's eyebrows rose.

"You know how she loves attention. Well, she's getting plenty of it now."

"Horses are smart, all right, but I don't know that even Cinnamon could figure that out."

Virginia shrugged. But she couldn't help feeling a little irritated with Cinnamon. Was it possible? Could a horse fake an injury just to get attention? Virginia decided to keep a discreet eye on the little bay.

But though she spent more time at her kitchen window than she really could afford, Virginia never did catch the young filly moving about the corrals without the limp. It looked like Cinnamon really was in trouble after all.

CHAPTER 14

*V*irginia was surprised to hear a motorcar chugging its way up their driveway. The day was cold, and a brisk wind whipped up the snow and swirled it about before depositing it in fence-line drifts. No one traveled on such a day just for the pleasure of a drive. Virginia crossed to the window and pulled back the curtain. But she had to clean a spot in the frost before she could see who had pulled to a stop in front of their porch.

Her father stepped out of the car. This deepened the puzzled frown on Virginia's face. Her mother and father had been out to the Lewis farm just the evening before to "see how everyone's doing"—which Virginia immediately challenged. "You've come to see Martha," she had told her mother with a knowing smile. But now her father was back so soon. And he was alone.

Virginia was at the door before her father could knock.

He stepped into the kitchen, brushing snow from his

shoulders. "Brr. It's one nasty day out there" was his first observation.

"So what brings you out in it?" asked Virginia frankly. "There's not bad news, I hope."

"Well . . . it's not good news. But it could be worse, considering."

Virginia waited.

"Mrs. Withers had a bit of a fall."

"Was she out? In this?"

"No, no. She fell in her kitchen. The boy that shovels her walks found her. He always checks on her each time he comes round."

Virginia felt her legs go limp and dread creep up her spine. "Was she badly hurt?"

"Luke thinks her leg is broken. Just above the knee. He's at her place right now getting it set, but he thought you and Jonathan should know right away."

"Jonathan's in the barn," she said, turning toward the door.

"I'll go on down." Drew placed a hand on her arm, then turned to leave.

Jonathan hurried into town behind Drew. It was not the kind of day to risk taking babies out on the roads, Virginia had agreed, but it was difficult for her to wait for further news. It was after dark before she heard the car and looked out to see headlights faintly through the swirling snow. *Thank God he's home* was her silent prayer. On top of concerns for Grandmother Withers, she had been worried about her husband.

She pushed the kettle forward on the stove as she heard Jonathan stomping the snow from his boots on the porch. She was there to meet him at the door.

"How is she?"

He lifted his heavy jacket to the hook on the wall. "It's

broken, all right. But she is resting quite comfortably now, thanks to Luke."

"Oh, Jonathan."

Jonathan took her into his arms and patted her shoulder. Virginia felt too emotionally drained to even cry.

"Your mother says she'll look after her for the next few days."

What then? Virginia's mind jumped immediately to the future. *What will we do?* Her mother would not be able to keep that up for long. And there was no way Virginia could get into town daily.

Our town needs a hospital, her troubled thoughts swirled on. *It's too far to go to the city in cases like this. Occasional help certainly is not sufficient. She needs someone with her full time. . . .*

Virginia pulled away from Jonathan with a sigh and reached to brush a strand of hair from her eyes. "I've got the water hot. You must be chilled."

"Has Martha had her last feeding yet?"

His query, so totally off the subject at hand, surprised her. "No. She'll want to eat once more. I'm surprised she hasn't wakened yet."

"Good," he said and crossed to the baby's cradle. He lifted her gently and headed for the rocking chair. Virginia decided that the weightless bundle in his arms would bring him far more comfort and warmth than a cup of hot chocolate. She moved the kettle to the back of the stove.

———

After many discussions of the situation, there seemed to be nothing else to do but to move Mrs. Withers in with them. Jonathan went to town and packed up her bed and dresser into the wagon. They pushed together living room furniture and squeezed the items in where the fire would keep the invalid warm and Virginia would not be required to run up and down the stairs.

The coming days were not going to be easy, Virginia knew, but she was hopeful that the leg would heal quickly and things would return to normal. She had agreed with Jonathan that there was really no choice about the matter. Virginia's mother had bundled the indoor violets against the winter weather and rushed them next door to the warmth of her own kitchen. With no one to see to the fires in Mrs. Withers' little home over the weeks ahead, the violets could not stay on her kitchen shelf and wouldn't have survived the chilly transport to the farm.

In the days that followed, Virginia tried to present a cheery face when she interrupted a huge pile of laundry to get Mrs. Withers another pain pill or laid a not-too-patient Martha aside, half-fed, to assist with the commode. By the end of each day her back ached from lifting, running, and scrubbing.

To make matters worse, Mindy resented this further intrusion in the family. Her temper tantrums increased, leaving Virginia at wit's end to know when to discipline and when to cuddle. If only she could foresee what Mindy really needed.

Fairly soon, she was noticing that Jonathan could walk out the door each morning to the reasonably peaceful barn with only half-broken horses to face. She found herself envying him. At least he had a sort of routine. At least the animals he'd face were somewhat predictable. At least they didn't throw themselves on the floor and kick and scream, or cry when they needed to be fed, or ask sweetly, "Would you mind, dear?" or "Could you please bring me. . . ?"

He didn't freeze his fingers hanging wet laundry out on frozen clotheslines or have to duck diapers hanging across the kitchen over the heat of the stove. He didn't have to run to keep two fires burning or have to remember to punch down the bread dough in between washing one pile of dishes and making another with the next meal's preparations.

There were days when Virginia was afraid she would snap. There was too much to do and too little energy to get it all done. And soon little niggling resentments began to wear down her already depressed spirit.

Why was she the one so overburdened with others' care? Why did Jonathan's life seem to continue on as before? Oh, it was true that he had assumed some of the care of the child they had taken in. But why shouldn't he? It had been his decision as much as Virginia's. They both had known they couldn't stand by and let little Mindy be placed in some institution for unwanted or homeless children.

And he had wanted to be a father just as much as Virginia had looked forward to being a mother. Yet his only responsibility to the baby seemed to be to rouse her from a nap each evening so he might have the pleasure of holding her for a brief time. And it was, after all, his grandmother whose bed filled their living room so there scarcely was walking space. Why was it Virginia who ran all the invalid's errands, maintained her care?

The wearier Virginia became, the more unfair to her it all became. And the more unfair it felt, the more her limited energy was depleted.

———

"Mindy, could you get Grandma the book off that table?" Virginia heard Grandmother Withers ask.

"Why?" asked the little girl sullenly. "You get it."

"I can't."

"Why?"

"Because my leg is broken."

There was a moment's silence. Virginia held her breath, wondering if she should intervene.

"What's 'broken' mean?"

"It means the bone broke when I fell."

"What *you* got bones in your leg for? Chickens got bones."

"So do I. So do you."

"No, I don't."

"Yes, you do. If God hadn't put bones in your legs, you wouldn't be able to walk. Or run or jump."

The child seemed to think about that for a few moments. "You got them," she replied, "and you can't."

"I could if it wasn't broken."

"Make it unbroke then."

"I am. That's what's happening while I'm in bed. I'm letting the leg get unbroke. This is the only way to fix it. To let it heal."

Again there was silence.

"How long's it gonna take?" asked Mindy, her voice holding just a trace of sympathy.

"It takes a long time."

"When it gets better will you get up?"

"Yes."

Another thoughtful silence.

"When you get up will you go back to your flower home?"

"Yes."

Virginia heard Mindy stir off the rocking chair.

"I'll get it for you this once." It seemed to be quite a concession. "But your leg better get unbroke quick."

But in the days that followed, Mindy did agree to get this or reach that for Grandmother Withers. Virginia felt that the little girl, in her own way, was trying to heal up the broken limb so normal routine could return to the household as quickly as possible.

In spite of all of Jonathan's ministrations, Cinnamon continued to limp. It became clear that she would not be ready for the spring sale. Virginia herself held back from asking the obvious question: If the filly didn't sell, what would they do to meet their financial obligations? The concern gnawed away at Virginia day after day. Would they be able to make it? If they paid the bank loan, would they have enough left over to carry them through the months ahead? It was true they were able to supply most of their own food. The farm produce made them almost self-sufficient, but there were other needs. Could new terms be negotiated with the local banker? Just how much would this set them back? Would they need to forfeit their future in order to protect the present? Virginia's worry about their financial uncertainties added to her own inner heaviness.

They tried to carry on as usual, but she could feel the tensions affecting the entire household. Even Mindy seemed to notice it. Virginia would turn from her baking to see the little child studying her face intently as though trying to sort through what was wrong. Mindy watched Jonathan with the same puzzled expression. It made it even harder to push the troubling thoughts aside and pretend that there was nothing the matter.

Mrs. Withers must have felt it too, though Virginia and Jonathan made a point of not discussing any difficulties except in late-night chats in the confines of their own bedroom. In the evenings while he sat in the rocker with baby Martha and talked of the day's simple happenings, the elderly lady began to ask gently prying questions of Jonathan.

Virginia, fashioning a knitted sock in a nearby chair, listened in amazement at how much Grandmother Withers seemed to already know when they had said nothing. And Jonathan answered each of her questions honestly without elaboration. Yes, it had already been a long winter, but it wasn't over yet. Yes, it would be some time until their own pastureland produced enough grass for the horses. Yes, he was rationing out the hay, hoping it would see them through. Yes, it was terribly disappointing to have his prime animal unfit for sale. Yes, he had counted on the income. No, he hadn't talked to the banker as yet, but he figured to go on into town as soon as there was a break in the weather.

Virginia's knitting needles clicked on. She wondered just what that next trip into town would be able to achieve. She also thought that it probably was easier for Jonathan to answer questions from his grandmother than from her.

———

It was not good news that Jonathan brought back from town. The banker had agreed to a three-month extension on the loan payment. That was the best he could possibly do.

But they needed more time than that—at least until the next spring sale when additional two-year-olds would be ready, eight prime young horses. Jonathan was pleased with the new lot. They were training well and were magnificent animals.

And a number of the mares would soon be dropping new spring foals. They should care for the needs of another year. After this year, things should ease off. The farm should be able to pay for itself. If they just could figure out something for that looming bank payment. . . .

At the breakfast table Virginia, who was facing the kitchen window, noted a strange red glow in the sky. "Must be quite a sunrise," she observed. "Sky's red clear to the west."

"Not time for the sun to be coming up yet," Jonathan said with a frown. The sight brought him quickly up out of his chair, his face paling even before he reached the window. Virginia saw his whole body go tense.

"What is it?" She was rising to her feet when he whirled around.

"The haystack's on fire."

He was gone from the house without even stopping for his jacket.

There was no use trying to fight it. The flames had gotten too far in the dry hay, and there was no water except what could be coaxed from the pump in the yard. All they could do was stand and watch it burn while horses in nearby corrals whinnied and blew and raced around the fence in sheer terror. Jonathan sought to quiet them, but even his familiar voice had little effect. Virginia wondered if they, too, knew the consequence of this disaster.

Helplessly she returned to the house, feeling sick inside. *Why don't we just give up? Sell the farm and move back into town?* She knew Jonathan could make a living in carpentry. He had proven his skills in building their house. Surely . . . surely carpentry would be much more reliable than raising horses. And he would have more time too. He might even have a chance to be a real husband and father. Not a visitor at the end of a long day. Not someone so weary that all he was able to do was sit by the fire and rock his child. *Yes*, decided Virginia, *that is what we must do*. She would talk to Jonathan about it. Surely he would agree.

———

But Jonathan did not agree. He said very little while Virginia laid out her solution to all their problems as they lay beneath the warmth and safety of their homemade quilt. But she could tell by his silence and the stiffness of his body that he was not in agreement.

For a moment she felt deep frustration and wanted to tell him that he was being stubborn. He was refusing to consider his family. *What is for our good?* her mind clamored. But she knew that was unfair. Jonathan had always thought about his family.

But it did not seem that he intended to be reasonable now. Was his dream too hard to let go? Couldn't he see that it was not weakness that led one to admit defeat, but strength?

She tried again. He had a goodly amount of assets out in his barns. If he sold the farm and all his horses, and if they were worth as much as he thought they were, he'd be able to pay off their debts and still have a sizable amount to put toward a house in town. It was the only sensible thing for them to do. Why couldn't he see that? Virginia presented her arguments, her voice getting a little higher pitched with each new expression of her position.

When Jonathan seemed unwilling to either refute or concede, Virginia turned her back to him. There was no use discussing it further. Hot tears fell into her goose-down pillow. What was the use? She had tried so hard to be a dutiful wife. To support her husband in his dream, his venture. Here she was, burdened with the care of family. Family that really should not have been her sole responsibility. And carrying most of it alone, while Jonathan escaped to his animals. Maybe she was the one who should be moving back into town.

Virginia chastised herself for even thinking such a thought, but her tears only increased. It seemed that her lot was a very heavy one. It would have helped to have had the comfort of Jonathan's arms.

CHAPTER 15

*T*he next morning, Virginia found it hard to rise from her bed. Jonathan was already gone from their room. Virginia could hear Mindy's voice drifting up the stairs. She was not sure if the child was speaking with Jonathan or Grandmother Withers. She could not pick out the words, only the rise and fall of the little girl's voice. Martha, who had been fed at four, slept on. Virginia fervently hoped she would not awaken again until the family had been served their breakfast.

She forced herself from the warmth of the covers and reached a reluctant foot out to the rag rug by the bed. She wished she did not need to face this day. She wondered just how Jonathan would greet her after their disagreement of the night before.

Slowly she dressed and descended the steps. Jonathan had already left for the barn. It was to Grandmother Withers that the young child was talking.

". . . and then Papa said it was only a dream and I should go back to sleep again."

"Did you?"

"No, I couldn't. I was scared. I thought the fire was gonna get me."

"But the fire was way out on the other side of the corrals."

"That's where it was before. But it might come here."

So Mindy had had a nightmare concerning yesterday's fire. Virginia had not heard her during the night. She slept more soundly than she had supposed. Jonathan must have been up with her. She wondered how long his rest was interrupted before the child was able to go back to sleep. And now he was up again. It likely had been a rather short night for Jonathan.

Virginia nodded a good-morning to Grandmother Withers and passed on through to the kitchen. She had to get breakfast on the table. Jonathan would soon be in from chores.

Jonathan was later than usual. By the time he came in, Martha was awake and insisting on being fed. Mindy, too, was whining, saying her tummy hurt. Virginia wondered if Grandmother Withers would start in next. She hurried to get the bedridden woman's breakfast in to her, then on the table for the rest of the family.

When Jonathan finally arrived, he looked as though he had already worked a long day. Neither seemed much in the mood for conversation, and they ate their meal in silence. Jonathan was starting to rise from the table when he looked across at Virginia. "I've been thinking about what you said," he began, his voice even and controlled. "If that's what you want, that's what we'll do. It'll take time to work it out, so I have to ask for your patience."

And then he rose and left, his face blank and unreadable.

Now you are being reasonable, Virginia's heart cried. But a sadness tugged at her as well. Rather than feeling triumph over winning, she felt a little sick inside. She knew that this was not what Jonathan would choose to do. She knew how much the horses meant to him, this enterprise in which he had invested so much time and care. She felt this was the only option open to the family, but if she could express her empathy for the deep hurt she knew he was feeling, it would be so much easier. In his eyes he had failed his family. In his eyes . . . But her tongue wouldn't move, and her throat felt parched. She said nothing, only stared at the closed door. Then she buried her face in Martha's soft blankets and wept.

But what else could they do? They could not pile up debt. The lost foal of the year before, the lost sale of Cinnamon, now the fire that took all the feed except what was in the barn loft—any one loss, they might have survived, but they had such a slim margin that the combination of the three was too much. Wasn't it?

Maybe they could sell off part of the stock. Maybe cut the size of the herd down to half the brood mares. But even Virginia, who knew only a little about raising animals, realized it would take a long, long time to build the herd up again. In the meantime, there would not be enough profit to sustain them. Jonathan had carefully worked out his plan. He knew just how many animals he had to have in the stalls, how many he would need to sell each spring. How much he would need to set aside each year for other expenses. Jonathan had all the figures in the book that he kept in the desk drawer. The precarious balance of accounts had already been destroyed. Jonathan had not counted on so many setbacks in such quick succession.

Virginia went about the tasks of her day with a heavy heart. So much so that small Mindy asked midmorning, "Mama, are you scared of the fire too?" Virginia could only nod. Yes. Yes, she was scared of the fire. Scared of what it would do to the family.

In the afternoon, Grandmother Withers and Mindy both took naps, and thankfully, small Martha joined them, leaving Virginia free to get to some long overdue household tasks.

She was rinsing the new butter that lay in a golden lump at the bottom of the churn when there was a knock on the door. "Who on earth. . . ?" But before she could even complete her thought the door opened and there stood Jenny.

Virginia blinked, unable to believe her eyes. The next moment a surprising thought flashed through her mind: *Well, at least you will be able to take care of your child now.* But her immediate inner response was that Mindy was no longer Jenny's. She had forfeited her right to the child. Mindy was theirs now. Hers and Jonathan's. They could not give her up. Surely Jenny would not ask them to. Surely not. Certainly they were still struggling. Still trying to work through Mindy's problems. But they were hopeful. They—

"Jenny," said Virginia, interrupting her own internal dialogue. Her voice sounded flat to her ears. "Come in."

"I'm in," replied Jenny with no apology.

Virginia found herself wondering if Mindy had awakened. How would she respond to her mother? In jubilation? With shyness? Fear? Virginia had no way of knowing.

Virginia did not know what to say, so she stood, butter churn still in her hands, mouth half-open.

"Guess you're a little surprised?" said Jenny.

Virginia finally was able to move. She crossed to the cupboard and set the churn near the water pail. "Yes," she managed. "Yes, I guess I am."

"I don't blame you. It's been a long time."

"Yes. It has." Virginia removed the lid from the churn and poured the fresh buttermilk into a pitcher. Then she dipped cold water from the pail and poured it over the yellow ball of soft butter and began to work out the butter-milk with a spoon, turning it over and over, pressing, squeezing. She poured the used water into the slop bucket and put on fresh to begin the process all over again.

"I'll just be a minute," she said over her shoulder. "Then I'll fix coffee. Take off your wraps and have a chair."

Jenny removed her coat and tossed it over a kitchen chair.

"How did you come?"

"The train. Then I caught a ride with a neighbor who dropped me off here."

Silence.

"How's Mindy?"

"She's . . . she's really grown."

"Good."

Silence again.

"How's Hayden?"

There was no response for such a long time that Virginia looked up from kneading the butter. Jenny sat, head in hands, looking pale and worn. "Trouble again?" asked Virginia candidly but with sympathy.

Jenny nodded.

Virginia set aside the butter without working in the salt and went to put on the coffeepot. Jenny needed its warmth—for body and soul.

"Do you want to talk?" asked Virginia, wiping her hands on her apron as she moved to the table and took a chair opposite Jenny.

Jenny looked up. She blinked back her tears and shook her head with determination. "It worked for a while."

"Then?"

"He . . . he sort of . . . came and went. This time he says he's gone for good. He's asking for . . . a divorce."

"You're going to give him one?"

"I don't know. I don't know. I still . . . He's everything

I ever wanted, Virginia. Everything."

Then you have set your sights awfully low, Virginia wanted to say, but she did not.

"So I've come to you," went on Jenny with a forced laugh. "Run back to good old Virginia whenever you need a favor."

"A favor?"

Jenny flushed. *At least she has that much decency*, thought Virginia. *She can blush about using me.*

Jenny nodded. "Just this once."

"And that favor is?" prompted Virginia when Jenny did not go on.

Jenny's flush deepened. She toyed with the rings on her fingers, seeming embarrassed to speak. At last she took a deep breath. "Well . . . you know how you are always saying that . . . that God answers prayer."

Virginia's heart skipped. Was Jenny finally at the point where she was willing to turn to God? Virginia could feel her eyes begin to moisten. She nodded. "He does," she said softly.

"Well I—I want to ask you to pray for me."

Oh, Jenny. You don't know how I've prayed to hear you speak those words, cried Virginia's heart.

Jenny went on, "I want you to pray that God will bring Hayden back."

Virginia was dumb struck.

"What? What do you want me to pray?"

"I need him, Virginia. I really do!"

Virginia felt sick at heart. She managed to move from her chair and go to the stove to slide back the boiling coffeepot.

"Will you?" prompted Jenny.

Virginia shook her head. "I don't know, Jenny. It's . . ."

"You always said that He answers. You—"

"He does," Virginia interrupted.

"But He won't do this. Not for me. Is that what you're saying?"

"I don't know. What—"

"Because I'm a sinner?" pressed Jenny. "Is that why He won't answer my prayer? I'm not praying, Virginia. *You're* praying. You're not a sinner. He'd answer you. That's why I came. I tried it. Honestly. I tried to pray, but He wouldn't answer me."

Virginia looked up from pouring the two cups of coffee. She was still shaking her head. She still felt weak and pale. "Would *you?*" she asked frankly.

Jenny looked puzzled.

"If you were God? Would you answer a prayer like that?"

Jenny remained silent.

"Would you give a person this kind of request, knowing full well that she would just use prayer to get what she wanted and then turn her back on you again?"

"Well . . . I . . ."

"That's what you intend to do, isn't it, Jenny? You want God to bring Hayden back. Back to you so the two of you can continue on as you left off. Living a life that leaves God out. Doing exactly what you want to do. Ignoring your conscience. Is that what you plan?"

Jenny tossed her tangled curls of fading red hair and shot Virginia a look of total contempt. "I guess I don't need you to tell me how to live my life, Virginia."

She rose from the chair and crossed to the window, her back stiff with anger.

For a moment Virginia wished she had not spoken so bluntly. It had accomplished nothing except to make Jenny upset with her. Virginia was always saying the wrong thing. If only she could take back her words. Jenny would never be won.

Suddenly Jenny whirled around. "Okay. So you're

right. I wouldn't change my life. I don't want to change my life. If I did . . . I'd just lose Hayden all over again. And I like my life . . . most of the time. If Hayden would come back, I'd be happy. At least I would be happier than I am now. But if your God . . . if He's unwilling to help a person who's down . . . then I don't know if I want anything to do with Him anyway. Who needs Him?"

"I do," said Virginia with emphasis. "I do. And He does help a person who's down. All the time. We all have our down times, Jenny. God has never failed me at such a time. But He's not there to be used at our own whim or fancy for our own purposes. That's not God. That would be a . . . a wish fairy, a year-round Santa Claus."

"Then I . . ."

"God is far more interested in your spiritual being than your state of happiness. He wants your life to be much more than a continual party with a hangover in the morning."

Jenny was trembling as she moved back to the chair at the table. Virginia did not know if it was from anger, disappointment, or conviction.

Virginia carried the two cups of coffee to the table and put them down. She took the chair opposite her longtime friend and reached for Jenny's hand.

"Oh, Jenny, if you only could understand how good life can really be."

Jenny's head jerked up. "That's easy for you to say. You were raised in a real home. Your mother didn't run away. Your father didn't come home drunk. Well, mine did and I can't change that. I've been trapped by it. All my life I've had to live with it. Can't you see that, Virginia? I am what I am because that is what life has made me. I can't change that. I've had no choice."

"That's where you're wrong. As long as there's a God, there's a choice. Think about it, Jenny. He created us, and one of the things He placed inside us is free choice. He will not let that be taken from us. Not by life, not by others. Not by Satan himself. He has given us choice. It's a wonderful gift. Think about it. No matter what life hands us, we still have choice.

"Oh, we can't always choose our circumstances—and I admit that yours have been unfair and cruel—but we can choose our response to them. We can choose."

"It's too late now. I'm . . . I've already made my choices. I'm trapped now. I can't change. What's done is done."

"You're wrong, Jenny. You still have a choice—even now. You can listen to your heart and ask for God's forgiveness—let Him change you. Or you can choose to go on, caught in the power of your habits and your sin. You still have that choice. That power has been given to you. No one—listen to me—no one can ever say, 'It's beyond my power to choose.' They might feel that way, but even that statement makes a choice. They are giving in when they could be reaching out and letting God give them freedom."

Jenny looked agitated. She pulled her hand away from Virginia and wiped a wrist across her eyes. "It's too late."

"It's only too late if you decide it's too late," insisted Virginia. "You choose."

"I couldn't do it on my own."

"He's not asking you to. He'll be there for you."

Jenny shook her head. "Why do you always manage to get me in such a mess, Virginia?" she asked almost crossly. "I came here looking for help, and all you give me is a lecture."

"If you could only see the help that is available," said Virginia. "But I can't make that decision for you. How I wish I could, but the choice is yours."

"I'll . . . think about it."

This was not what Virginia had hoped for, but at least it was a start. It was the first time Jenny had ever promised to give any kind of consideration to the need of her soul.

———

Jenny stayed with them for three days. In all that time Mindy ignored her. And Jenny did not try to make up to the little girl. Virginia did not know if she was sad or glad at the lack of interchange between the two.

"Do you want to tell Mindy that you are her real mama?" she had asked Jenny as they sat before the fire on the first evening. Mindy had already been tucked in for the night.

Jenny had looked up. She shook her head slowly. "I don't think that would be true," she said at last. Then, "From what I've seen, you are her real mama. I just gave her birth."

Virginia felt tears burning her eyes.

"She has changed," went on Jenny. "You've been good for her, Virginia. You and Jonathan. I think it's best to leave things that way. It would only stir things up if we were to talk about me as her mama. Perhaps when she's older. We'll see."

So they had left it. Mindy did not ask questions concerning Jenny, and no one volunteered the information.

On the third day, Jenny packed her case and asked Jonathan for a ride to town. It nearly broke Virginia's heart. She was filled with sadness that Jenny was choosing the wrong way again.

"You promised to think about what I said," she reminded Jenny as she gave her a good-bye embrace.

Jenny nodded, and then she was gone.

CHAPTER 16

$\mathcal{V}$irginia could not sleep that night. She went over and over her conversations with Jenny. Two things troubled her: Jenny's refusal to see that there was hope and freedom in accepting God's forgiveness and deliverance from her bondage, and then her own words, which spoke truth to her heart. She thoroughly believed all that she had said to Jenny. Yet why was she unable to live it? We have choices, she had explained to her old friend, not always over our circumstances but over our attitude toward them. Yet here she was locked in despair and depression over her own situation. Virginia knew that it didn't make sense. Either she believed what she said, or she did not. And if she believed it, she ought to be able to live it.

On through the night hours she struggled. She would have left her bed and gone downstairs to pray, but she was afraid she would disturb Grandmother Withers. So she stayed where she was, hoping her restlessness did not bother Jonathan.

Tears dampened her pillow. She was a hypocrite. She had told Jenny that God was there. That He helped her through times of trial. That there was always hope, for there was always choice. God did not allow that to be taken away. And where there was choice, one could reach out, could go beyond the bonds of circumstance, could find a way of escape from the temptation of accepting defeat. She wasn't the first person in the world to have a difficult lot. Nor would she be the last. They weren't the first couple ever to face economic hardship. Yet here she was wallowing in self-pity. Angry with Jonathan for things beyond his control. Resentful of a grandmother for breaking her leg and causing more stress on an already burdened household. It was ridiculous—her behavior, her attitude. Why did she strike out at those she loved? Let bitterness gnaw away at her soul? She knew better. She knew she had chosen foolishly. She was creating much of her own trouble.

Virginia could stand it no longer. She slipped from her bed and knelt on the rag rug. With tears of repentance she began to pray. The night air was cold and she shivered against the chill, but she scarcely noticed. She was far too intense in making peace with her God.

As she prayed, her heavy burden lifted. She would not give in to despair again. There was a way out of their present situation. God was faithful. Perhaps it would indeed mean leaving the farm, but she would no longer try to manipulate things her way. She and Jonathan together would work through what to do. She would tell him first thing in the morning that she would stop her stewing and fretting and leave the final decision with him and with God.

Virginia rose from her kneeling position. But before she went back to bed, she crossed the hallway and entered

Mindy's room. Again she knelt. "God, this is your child. I give her to you in a new way tonight. Give me love and patience and understanding . . . and wisdom, Lord. I need wisdom. But help me to remember that you are even more concerned about this little one than I am. You lead her, Lord. You work in her little heart and soul to free her of her past and lead her into a bright future full of promise and right choices. Help me not to fret and stew and confine her to the person that I think she should be but give you the freedom to work in her life."

Silently Virginia tiptoed down the stairs. She crossed to the bed where Grandmother Withers' regular breathing told her that she was sleeping soundly. "Lord," she prayed silently, "thank you for Grandmother Withers. I love her. She has been a blessing in my life. Help me to be patient and loving. Help her leg to heal. May she be able to be active again. To enjoy her garden. To work in her own kitchen. But until that time, Lord, may she find happiness here with us. May she feel wanted and loved . . . and even needed in this home. Thank you for bringing her here to us."

Virginia made her way back up the stairs. She was beginning to feel the cold of the house on a winter's night. But before returning to the warmth of her bed she stopped at Martha's cradle. The glow from the moonlight cast a soft shine over the baby's features. One small fist lay curled by her cheek. She pursed her lips and mimicked sucking, and Virginia knew it would not be long before she would be wanting to nurse again. Virginia's hand reached down to rest on the blankets. "God, thank you for our beautiful, healthy baby. She has already brought us so much joy. Help me to be the mother you intended for her. Give me wisdom and patient love all of her days as I seek to guide her to you. Help me to live what I believe so that she, too, might become a believer. Amen."

With one final pat of the baby's blankets, Virginia wiped her tears and turned to her bed. But before she crawled once more beneath the blankets she knelt again.

"Lord, I thank you for Jonathan. For his love. His gentleness. His strength. Thank you for bringing him here to share my life. Be with him through this present difficulty. Give him wisdom about what is to be done. Help me to support him in that decision—whatever it might be. Help me to remember that we are a couple. That we walk together. As a team, Lord. Not as two separate individuals, but as you have admonished, 'In honour preferring one another.' Thinking of one another. Supporting one another. Living for one another. Then we will find the happiness that you have for us. I love him, Lord. Deeply. Bless him—even as he sleeps. Amen."

Virginia climbed carefully back into bed, trying not to disturb Jonathan. He needed his rest. She needed hers also. Tomorrow would be another long day. She was ready now to sleep.

———

"Grandmother says she wants to go to town," Virginia told Jonathan as he hung up his jacket.

"To town?" He turned, sounding as surprised as Virginia had been when Grandmother Withers had made her request.

Virginia nodded.

"Why on earth? How does she expect to manage that?" he asked, moving to the corner basin to wash up before breakfast.

Virginia shook her head. "I've no idea. But she insists there is something she needs to attend to."

Jonathan's voice lowered. "How will we even get her to the car? That cast is nearly as heavy as she is."

"Well—we must try to find a way. It seems important to her."

Previously Virginia would have chafed over the unreasonable request. This morning, after her night of prayer, she felt much more calm. More serene. Even this strange notion of Grandmother Withers' could not disturb her.

"Any ideas?" Jonathan splashed the warm water over his face and neck and sudsed his hands thoroughly. He reached for the towel.

"Not really. Maybe the two of us could carry her. That's how you and Father got her in here."

Jonathan nodded. "I'll talk to her."

But at the present, Mindy was talking to her—an occurrence that was happening much more frequently of late. Virginia could hear the small voice from the living room and guessed that she was likely leaning up against the bed where the woman rested.

". . . and I used to feed the chickens—all by myself."

"But you don't anymore."

"Nope."

"Why not?"

"Because. Because I don't want to be a help to Mama."

Virginia nearly stopped in her tracks. So the child had a reason. A reason that she was fully aware of. She had stopped doing her chores as punishment to Virginia for bringing a new baby into the home. *My, but we do start making choices early*, thought Virginia with a wry smile.

But Grandmother Withers was speaking. "Did it make you feel happier not to help Mama?"

There was silence, then a reluctant "I was still mad."

"Don't you miss saying good morning to the chickens and the kittens? And Murphy? I'll bet they've been missing you."

"Maybe," conceded Mindy.

"Maybe you should feed them this morning and see if it makes them happy."

"What about Mama?"

"I think it would make your mama happy too."

"But she's gonna keep Martha."

"Martha is part of the family. We can't give Martha away. Did you see Martha smile when you walked by her cradle yesterday?"

"No."

"I did. I think Martha likes her big sister. She . . ." The porridge needed stirring. Virginia could not catch the rest of the conversation. But she was not too surprised when after breakfast Mindy slid from her chair and announced that she would be feeding the chickens.

———

It took them both to get Grandmother Withers out to the motorcar. Jonathan had pulled it in as close to the steps as he could. Even so, it took some effort to get the elderly woman out of her bed, through the kitchen, and across the porch and into the back seat. They were finally able to cradle their arms beneath her, forming a seat of sorts to carry her. Virginia felt certain that the whole effort must have been very difficult for Grandmother Withers as well, but the woman bit her lip and endured whatever pain was involved.

Thankfully it was a rather pleasant day. There was no wind blowing, and the sun's bright rays even held the hint of coming spring. Virginia took deep breaths of the fresh, clear air. It seemed like a long time since she had been outdoors other than to hang laundry or feed the small animals. Today she would go to town too. So far Grandmother had not disclosed her destination, but they assumed she wanted to check on her little house.

All four of them had to crowd into the front seat because Grandmother Withers needed the back seat to make room for her cast. Virginia held baby Martha and pressed Mindy up close against her side so Jonathan would have room to shift the gears.

Even though the day was sunny, the trip into town was a chilly one. The car heater tried valiantly to keep the temperature comfortable. Virginia rapidly tapped her feet now and then to try to keep them warm and was glad they'd had the foresight to tuck Grandmother Withers in with blankets.

When they neared the town limits, Grandmother spoke. "Take me round on Fourth Street. To Mrs. Cadbury's place." Jonathan turned in his seat to look back at his grandmother. Virginia feared he might drive them into the ditch.

Mrs. Cadbury was the widow lady whom Jonathan had hired to care for his grandmother before her fall. "Now, Grandmother. You're not thinking of doing something silly, are you?" he asked. "You know that Mrs. Cadbury only has three days a week free."

"I know that."

Surely Grandmother Withers was not about to insist on going back to her own house with her leg still in the cast. It was unthinkable. She would never be able to manage on her own, and they would be worried day and night.

"You wouldn't. . . ?" began Jonathan.

"No. I wouldn't."

"Good."

Jonathan was able to return his attention to driving.

They drove to Mrs. Cadbury's tall brownstone house and struggled once more to get Grandmother Withers out of the car. Mindy was assigned the task of making sure Martha did not roll from the car seat onto the floor. She took the job most seriously. "Don't you wiggle, Martha,"

Virginia heard her say. "You'd get a bump."

It seemed to take a long time to maneuver Grandmother up the steps and into Mrs. Cadbury's living room. All three of them were exhausted by the time the task was completed. "That's just fine," Grandmother Withers said with a relieved sigh as she was settled on the settee, a footstool propping up her leg cast. Mrs. Cadbury bustled about preparing tea for her unexpected guest.

"You can come back for me in an hour," Grandmother told the two.

They exchanged puzzled looks, but Jonathan gave a nod and Virginia turned to go, anxious to get back to the car and the children.

"No," Grandmother Withers called just before they stepped through the door. "You'd better make that two hours."

"Now, what is that all about?" Jonathan asked as they walked down the steps.

"I've no idea."

"She didn't say anything?"

"Not a word—except that it was urgent to get to town."

"Grandmother wouldn't be owing her money."

Virginia knew that was true. Jonathan had paid to have the lady's help for his grandmother.

Jonathan shrugged. "Maybe she was just feeling lonesome. Needed a tea party."

Virginia thought back over the days that had passed since Grandmother Withers had been with them. She had cared—sometimes reluctantly—for the older woman's needs. But she certainly had not provided tea parties. Guilt stained her cheeks. She would try harder to make things pleasant in the future.

"Jonathan," she said, slipping her hand into his. "I . . . I know this isn't the time nor place. But . . . I'd really like to talk. Sometime soon. I've . . . been a bit difficult to live with. Jenny's visit . . . well . . . it sort of helped me work it out. Made me face some things. I'd like to talk about it."

She felt Jonathan's hand tighten on hers.

"I was wrong about selling the farm," she continued. "The horses. There must be another way."

"Virginia, I think you might have been right. I only have feed for another few days."

"But there must be some way. Something we can do."

"It's okay."

"We'll pray about it."

"I've been praying about it. Lots. It'll be okay. I can get along without my horses. Honest."

"I . . . I hope you won't have to."

"Well, I'll talk with the banker and see if he has any ideas for how we can work it out. Maybe we won't need to lose everything. But if I do, it's enough to have you and Martha and Mindy. I can be happy with that."

Again his hand tightened on hers. That was the answer she needed.

When they reached the car, they found Mindy kneeling on the floorboards, leaning over Martha. The older child was chatting, the younger one smiling broadly. Virginia could not hear the conversation.

Upon seeing them, Mindy scrambled to her feet. "She didn't fall," she reported. "I asked her to lie still, and she did."

Then as an afterthought she added almost shyly, "I think she kinda likes me."

Jonathan drove Virginia and the children around to her folks. It had seemed forever since they had paid a call to her beloved childhood home. Belinda welcomed them with enthusiasm, and they laid aside wraps and settled in the kitchen while Jonathan went off to run some errands. Martha decided it was time to eat, so Virginia was occupied as her mother fixed tea.

"I sure wish I had someone to help me with the sugar bowl," Belinda said, her tone matter-of-fact. Mindy still had not gotten over her shyness with others, even her grandparents. But the small figure did silently walk over to the sugar bowl and carefully carry it to the table.

"Both of my granddaughters have grown so much! I can't believe it," exclaimed Belinda over and over with a quick pat on Mindy's shoulder and a touch on Martha's head.

"Jenny came again," Virginia reported. There wasn't much more that she could say with Mindy listening.

"How is she?"

"About the same, I guess."

"Still with her husband?"

"He's asked for a divorce. She's taking it pretty hard."

"Poor Jenny."

"We had a good talk. I was able to say some things I've wanted to say for a long time."

"Did it help?"

Virginia shifted Martha in her arms. She smiled. "Jenny . . . or me?"

Belinda raised her eyebrows in unspoken question.

"I discovered some things, Mama. I found I wasn't really living the faith I claimed. It got my attention—talking with Jenny. Here I was telling her about what she needed to do, when I was the one who really needed my own sermon. I decided I'd better do something about it."

Tears came to Virginia's eyes.

Belinda crossed to her daughter and placed her arms around her shoulders. It was awkward trying to embrace over the bundle in Virginia's arms. "Papa and I have been praying for you. You've had a heavy load. I don't know how you've managed."

"Not well, I'm afraid. But I will. From now on. I'm finally on the right track."

Martha squirmed and Mindy tugged at Belinda's sleeve. "Grandma, be careful. You're squishing our baby."

CHAPTER 17

Jonathan came back for Virginia and the girls before going over to pick up his grandmother. He had been to
the bank, but from the look on his face the results were not
good. He tried to hide it behind a cheery smile, but Virginia
was learning to read his eyes and could see the shadows.

"No help from the bank?" she asked quietly as they
climbed into the motorcar.

He shook his head. "Manager's a smart man," he said
with grudging admiration. "He says I have borrowed to
about my limit on the collateral I have. Living creatures—
like horses—are not very sound assets. Anything can happen to them."

"Anything can happen to anything, in this world."

Jonathan managed a chuckle.

"So how were my girls? Made Grandma Belinda
proud?"

Virginia beamed. "They were fine. Even let us have

our tea in peace. Mindy joined us, didn't you, Mindy? She liked Grandma's cookies."

"Martha's too little," Mindy informed her father.

"I'm sure Martha had her own party," said Jonathan with a teasing glance at Virginia.

"No, she didn't. She just nursed and slept."

Jonathan chuckled again.

Grandmother Withers seemed not the least anxious when they arrived back at Mrs. Cadbury's house. The two ladies appeared to have had a wonderful visit. Both were beaming good-naturedly and telling each other that they must do it again soon. Virginia pictured the difficulty in getting Grandmother Withers in and out of the motorcar and grimaced, but then remembered her self-made vow. If this kind of outing brought the older woman an afternoon of happiness, they could manage it again.

That evening, after the children had been put to bed, the three sat chatting beside the fire in the living room for a few minutes before closing up for the night.

After a pause in the conversation, Grandmother Withers said, "You must wonder about my insistence on going into town today."

Jonathan nodded. "Was a bit curious," he admitted. "It isn't like you to make sudden and unexplained requests."

"Well, I had to see Annie. That's Mrs. Cadbury."

Jonathan nodded and waited.

"In the past she had asked me now and then about my house. Had a son who was interested in buying. I always said no—enjoying the flowers like I did. But I've been lying here thinking for the last few days. I don't think I'll be able to tend the flowers much from now on. And it's far too much to expect you, Virginia, to run in and do it for me." She looked expectantly from Virginia to Jonathan. When neither spoke, she went on. "So I decided, with things like they are, I'd best just sell the house."

"You sold the house?" Jonathan could not believe his ears.

"I figured as soon as I get this cast off my leg, I'll take one of the rooms in the boardinghouse."

Virginia leaned forward in her chair. "Oh, Grandmother, you can't do that. Why . . ."

"Now, you just bear with me a minute. I know you'd have me on here, but I've a mind you've enough to do to care for your family. I've quite reconciled myself to it. Even looking forward to it in some ways. But I did have that attorney—your father, Virginia—write one thing into the sale agreement. You are to have slips from any of the plants in the yard that you've a liking for. You have three years to make up your mind."

"Oh, Grandmother" was all Virginia could say.

"And I've something for you, my boy," went on Grandmother Withers. "I know it's been tough going for you—getting started here and having the setbacks with the mare and the fire and all. I had the buyer make out two checks. One for me—so's I can be independent—and the other for you. I hope it will see you through until you get on your feet."

"I can't take that, Grandmother," Jonathan said before Virginia could even cry out in delight. His face was ashen, his jaw set.

"And why not?"

"It wouldn't be right. It's yours."

"Guess if it's mine I can do with it what I want."

"But . . ."

"Now, look here—do you think the few dollars that I got out of that little house will ever repay you for leaving your home in the West and coming back here to look after me? Do you think it will repay Virginia for emptying my slops and giving me sponge baths and putting up with a bedridden old woman when her own days were so busy she had to run to get through them? I know that you can't pay for love. And I know that this is not enough. I know that. But it's what I can do, and I want to do it. Please . . . please don't try to deny me that pleasure, Jonathan. It's the only way I have to say thank you."

Jonathan left his chair by the fire and crossed to the woman on the bed. He took her in his arms and held her close for a very long time. Virginia could tell by the slight shake of his shoulders that he was weeping. She bowed her head and let her own tears flow as she offered up a prayer of thanks.

———

Virginia could not believe the different atmosphere in the home. Or was the difference in her? She still had far more to do in a day than seemed possible to get done, but her attitude about the tasks, about each of the household members, had changed so much that even the toilsome duties took on new meaning. Many afternoons she took time for a special tea with Grandmother Withers. Sometimes they played a game of checkers. Sometimes they shared a book or worked on some new stitchery. Sometimes they just sat and sipped and chatted. Virginia was surprised at how refreshed she felt when she resumed her duties.

Jonathan made the trip in to see the banker and paid off his loan. He bought feed from a local farmer to get his stock through what remained of the winter, assured now that the two-year-olds would reach the spring sale in first-class shape. Mindy started making trips to the barn with Jonathan again, and she continued to feed the chickens, cats, and Murphy. "I think they did miss me," she told Grandmother Withers quite seriously. "The chickens all nodded their heads to say hello, and the kitties rubbed against my legs and purred. And Murphy—he was the happiest of all. He barked all over the place."

Mindy still had occasional reservations about baby Martha. But more and more she was sidling over to the baby's cradle to see if Martha would welcome her with a smile. Martha always did, gurgling and cooing and reaching for Mindy's braids. But now and then Martha's little fingers grabbed Mindy's nose or scratched a cheek, and then Mindy would cry out in accusation. Virginia tried to explain that the baby did not really mean to hurt. She just wanted to grab. She was still too little to understand about being gentle.

Mindy shook her head, angry and frustrated. "She should grow up," she said on one such occasion.

"She will. She grows a little every day."

———

When Dr. Luke announced that the cast could come off Grandmother Withers' leg, the entire family gathered around for the exciting event. Mindy's eyes grew big when he got out his tool. "Is he gonna cut Grandmother's leg off?"

Jonathan reached down and lifted her up. "Oh no. He's just going to get Grandmother's leg out of that nasty white house it's been living in for such a long time."

But when the procedure began, Mindy still looked doubtful. "I'm afraid he might," she said, scrunching tight her eyes and burying her face on Jonathan's shoulder.

Jonathan held her close until the last bit of sawing was complete and Grandmother's leg was free.

It looked whitened and withered and a bit sickly. Virginia wondered if the small child should see it and moved to stand in the way.

"Pass me those stockings, dear," Grandmother Withers requested and proceeded to quickly make the exposed leg match up with the other. "Now she can look."

Jonathan coaxed Mindy to take a look at her great-grandmother, and hesitantly the little girl lifted her head and opened her eyes. They widened in surprise.

"You've got two now," she said.

"Yes. Two."

"It's unbroke?"

"Unbroke."

"Get up." Apparently Mindy wanted to see if the fixed leg really worked.

"Oh, I can't get up quite yet, but very soon. Dr. Luke says I will need the help of a cane for a while."

"What's a cane?"

"A stick to help you walk."

From then on Mindy insisted on having her own stick. Jonathan cut one from a dead tree limb, peeling the bark off so it was smooth. She carried it with her wherever she went. When Grandmother Withers began walking about the house, cane in support, Mindy walked right beside her, leaning on her own stick and limping along in unison. Virginia smiled. They made quite a team.

———

Jonathan returned from the spring sale with a broad grin on his face. It sounded like his horses had made quite an impression on the buyers. "If they think those were something, they should see Cinnamon," said Virginia. Cinnamon still walked with a slight limp, but that did little to impair her beauty. She was a magnificent animal. Head high, eyes bright with intelligence and high spirits, mane and tail flowing, coat glistening in the unusual brownish bay color that had earned her name.

"I've been thinking about Cinnamon," said Jonathan

slowly. "You realize I would have sold her if she'd been sound."

Virginia nodded.

"Well, God does work in strange ways. I've a feeling that she's going to be worth a great deal more to me as a brood mare than she would have if I'd sold her this year."

Virginia's face reflected her surprise.

"I think we will be awful glad we've kept her. Just look at her out there." Jonathan nodded toward the corral where Cinnamon frolicked in spite of her limp. "Did you ever see such a wonderful horse? Match her up with Warrior and we'll have ourselves one first-rate animal."

Virginia nodded again. It was true. She smiled. God did work in mysterious ways.

"Look at them," Jonathan said, his arm around Virginia's waist as they looked out the window toward the corrals. "Each one prettier and spunkier that the last. We've got us some winners here, Virginia."

"You've also got yourself a powerful lot of work," said Virginia, the realist. It was going to take more hours than the day held to get all the new foals thoroughly broken and last year's yearlings ready for the next spring sale.

"That I have," admitted Jonathan. "But at least it's enjoyable work."

Virginia did not argue. She had learned that even though Jonathan was awfully busy, he was happy. And he brought that happiness with him every time he entered the house. The whole family benefited. She smiled. "So what are we naming this batch?"

"Thought you and Mindy might like the honors."

"That would be fun."

They settled on Copper, Midge, Minx, Captain, Star,

Dollie, Murphy, and Kitten, the final three names having been picked by Mindy. Jonathan accepted the names with a nod.

Throughout the long summer days, Jonathan worked from sunup to sundown. The family saw little of him, unless they looked out at the corrals where he worked with one horse or another. Virginia was glad to have Grandmother Withers for companionship. Together they managed to plant a garden, work up more flower beds, go into town for slips and roots from her previous home's garden, and in general learn to love and appreciate each other in new ways. Grandmother Withers had not mentioned the boarding-house again. Virginia was glad. With Grandmother there to read to a knowledge-thirsty Mindy or keep a watchful eye on a creeping Martha, Virginia was able to find time for a book now and then herself. In fact, it would be hard to think of their home without Grandmother Withers.

By August the elderly woman's leg was strong enough to do away with her cane. Mindy was disappointed. She liked their walking sticks and the bit of drama they provided. Grandmother now insisted that she could handle the stairs with no problem. Her bed and dresser were moved up the steps and into the spare room. Mindy was glad to have the story reader closer by, and Virginia was thankful to have the living room back into regular service.

Martha, who was now sleeping through the nights, was moved in to share Mindy's room. The little girl was delighted. Virginia often heard the two giggling together after they had been tucked in and wondered just who was entertaining whom and in what way. But she did not interfere, unless the laughter went on for too long. Then she would tiptoe to the door and admonish them both to quiet down and go to sleep.

Virginia often thought about Jenny. Where was she now and what were her circumstances? Virginia's heart ached for the lonely, desperate young woman. She inquired from time to time of Mr. Woods, but Jenny's father always answered the same way: He had heard nothing. Jenny had not even stopped to see him on her previous trips into town. He looked sad and lonely, and Virginia's heart grieved for him. He came to the farm on occasion to visit with Mindy, but so far the youngster refused to warm up to him. That grieved Virginia as well. She wished there were some way she could bridge the chasm between child and grandfather. He would smile patiently and remind Virginia that such relationships took time.

Mindy was still cautious and reserved with her other grandparents. Only Great-grandmother Withers seemed to have managed to win her over. *Perhaps that is what it takes*, thought Virginia. *Living in close proximity. Sharing a home and a storybook day after day.*

But Virginia could think of no way to repeat that with the other grandparents. They would just have to hope that time would accomplish the same effect.

———

Murphy's one bad habit was that he loved to chase the horses. Jonathan was forever shooing him away from the corrals.

To Murphy it all seemed to be a wonderful game. To the horses it was a great annoyance. "He's gonna get his head kicked in for sure if he doesn't stop that," Jonathan growled in disgust, going out once again to call in the dog.

But Murphy seemed to be very good at dodging the flashing hooves. He would sneak up behind an unsuspecting animal, dash in for a quick nip, then fall flat on his belly while the enraged animal lashed out above his head. Then would follow the wild chase as the horse took off at a gallop, Murphy hot on his heels, barking joyously that he had put the animal on the run. Virginia, watching the spectacle from her kitchen window, couldn't help but chuckle, then catch her breath in dismay. Jonathan was right. The dog was going to try it one time too often.

And it finally happened, just as Jonathan had predicted, only it wasn't Murphy's head that received the hoof but his right shoulder. Virginia was hanging out the wash and heard the crack all the way to the house. She lifted her head, and a few moments later, Jonathan came toward the house carrying the broken body of the hapless Murphy. "Well, he did it this time," said Jonathan. "Cricket really got him."

Virginia gasped and shook her head. "Oh no. Is he. . . ?"

"He's still breathing, but he's hurt pretty bad. His shoulder crunches when I move it."

"Oh no," Virginia said again.

"I think I'm going to have to put him . . ."

"Oh!" Virginia's hand went to her mouth and she could say no more.

"Where's Mindy?"

"She and Grandmother are in the garden."

Mindy. She loved Murphy. What would this do to dear Mindy? They couldn't risk another emotional setback for their still-vulnerable daughter.

"Oh, Jonathan. She will be heartbroken. Isn't there any way to save him? Can't we at least try?"

"He's pretty bad off. We don't want him to suffer." His expression was grim. "I'll take a look. Maybe give Danny a call. We'll see."

It was a faint hope, but Virginia clung to it as she watched Jonathan carry Murphy into his tool shed.

CHAPTER 18

$\mathscr{I}$’ve made him as comfortable as I can, but he’s in a lot of pain,” Jonathan whispered to Virginia. Mindy had still not heard of Murphy’s mishap. “I’m gonna run into town and see if I can get Danny on the phone.”

Virginia nodded. “Is there anything I can do for him while you’re gone?”

“I’ve confined him. He doesn’t like it much, but we can’t have him thrashing around. I’ll be back just as soon as I can.”

The time dragged until Virginia heard the car again. She hurried to the window to see a second motorcar pull in behind Jonathan. It was her uncle Luke, black doctor’s bag in hand. They went together into the tool shed. After waiting for what seemed forever, Virginia could stand it no longer. “Grandmother, I’m going out for a few minutes. Can you watch the children, please?”

Grandmother Withers nodded her assent and Virginia

hurried out. She found both men kneeling over a very still Murphy. He was so motionless Virginia was sure he was already gone. But Jonathan explained, "I couldn't reach Danny. Luke volunteered to take a look. He's given him something to ease his pain."

"He's in pretty bad shape, Virginia," said her uncle Luke. "The bone in his shoulder seems fragmented. There's no way I can just set it."

"Then . . . there's nothing we can do?"

"We can try surgery—it's the only way to find out the extent of bone chips or splinters. Maybe clean it up."

"Would it work?"

"Could. We'd have to wait and see what we find when we get in there."

"Then . . . let's."

"You're sure?"

"If you're willing . . . yes."

The two men exchanged looks. "We'd have to work on the kitchen table," said Luke.

Virginia nodded.

"I assume you don't want Mindy seeing this."

"No."

The silence hung around them as Virginia tried to figure out how to get the child away from the farm home. "How long will it take?"

"I can't say until I open him up. Could be an hour. Maybe longer."

"Could you take her picking flowers?" Jonathan wondered. "A walk to the creek? Berries? Anything."

"I couldn't be gone that long. Martha will want to eat. Maybe you . . ."

"But Luke needs help."

"I could help him," put in Virginia quickly. "If he just tells me what to do."

"Are you sure?" asked her uncle. "Surgery can get a bit messy."

"You might need to feed Martha at a crucial time," Jonathan reminded her.

"Well, we can't just let Mindy walk in and see her dog cut open—looking dead—on the kitchen table," she said.

"Maybe Grandmother can do something."

"Her leg still bothers her if she's on it for long."

"How about a picnic?" suggested Jonathan. "They could walk into the trees and have a picnic lunch and read books together."

It sounded like an idea that might work. Virginia hurried off to make the arrangements.

Grandmother Withers was quick to agree. "How will I know when it's safe to return?" she asked Virginia.

"We'll call. No, you might not hear that. We'll . . . Jonathan can shoot the rifle—three shots."

"He doesn't like to fire the gun around the horses."

"We'll blow the car horn. That's it. When you hear the car horn, you'll know it's over."

Mindy was excited to be heading off with Grandmother Withers for her own picnic in the woods. They carried a basket of sandwiches, cookies, and apples, and several books and a blanket.

"Bye, Mama," Mindy called over and over. They were going down the steps when Mindy exclaimed, "Let's take Murphy with us! He'd like a picnic."

"Not today," said Grandmother. "Today just you and I are going to have a picnic together. It's our own special Grandmother-and-Mindy picnic. Maybe next time we'll let Murphy join us."

Mindy was satisfied.

Virginia went right to work scrubbing the kitchen table. She shoved the kettle forward on the fire in case Uncle Luke would need hot water for sterilizing instruments, then pulled away the chairs so the men would have working room. Just then Jonathan entered the kitchen, the sedated dog in his arms.

Virginia was thankful her impulsive offer of help had not worked out. Murphy's shoulder had been shaved of hair and swabbed with disinfectant. The moment Luke made the first incision, Virginia felt the room begin to tilt. Before Luke had even exposed the broken bone she knew she was going to be sick. She rushed outside, where she lost her breakfast, then stood breathing in great gulps of fresh air.

But Martha would be waking soon to nurse. Virginia hated the thought of passing through the kitchen. The smell of the medications alone was likely to start her heaving again. At length she took herself firmly in hand and pushed open the door. Neither of the men, intent on their task, even looked up.

". . . pretty bad break," Luke was saying, "but it hasn't splintered as much as I had feared. There are bone chips that we'll . . ."

Virginia moved quickly out of hearing. She picked up Martha, even though the child had not yet stirred, and hurried up the stairs. She would spend the rest of her time out of earshot and away from the smells.

———

The sound of the car horn brought Grandmother Withers and Mindy back from their picnic. Mindy carried a bouquet of drooping wild flowers clutched tightly in her hand. It appeared they had been picked some time earlier, but Virginia fussed over them appropriately and placed them in a quart sealer of water. Mindy looked pleased.

"What's that funny smell?" asked the child, wrinkling her nose.

Virginia had scrubbed and scrubbed the kitchen table after the surgery but had been unable to get the smells of disinfectant and anesthetic from the room, now also joined by strong lye soap. But Mindy soon forgot about it when no one offered an answer to her question. Instead she announced, "We read and we read and we read," she enthused. "Over and over."

Grandmother Withers nodded, looking bemused. No doubt she had wondered if the car horn was ever going to sound.

How is Murphy? was the silent question in her eyes.

Virginia just nodded her head toward the tool shed. "Uncle Luke thinks there is a chance," she was able to say. Relief was evident in the older woman's face. "But we'll have to wait and see. The next twenty-four hours are the most crucial."

Jonathan spent most of the night in the tool shed. Virginia made several trips out to see how they both were doing. Murphy seemed to be resting fairly comfortably as long as Jonathan regularly gave the medication that Luke had left. Virginia greeted the sun over the eastern horizon with relief. Surely things would be better in daylight.

————

Mindy went do to her morning chores and came back in a rush.

"Murphy isn't out there!" she reported, eyes wide with concern. Jonathan and Virginia exchanged glances. He reached down and lifted the child up onto his lap.

"Murphy was hurt yesterday," he said carefully. "You know how Murphy likes to tease the horses?"

Mindy nodded solemnly.

"He did that yesterday and one of the horses kicked him."

"Hard?"

"Yes. Hard."

"Did he broke?"

"Yes. He broke the bone in his shoulder."

"Like Grandmother?"

"Well . . . not quite like Grandmother. Murphy's break was at a place where Dr. Luke couldn't put on a cast."

"Is he still broke?"

"Uncle Luke fixed him the best he could. But he is still real sick. We don't know yet if he'll get better."

"Can I see him?"

"He needs to be real quiet right now. Get lots of rest. Maybe later I can take you to see him."

"Where is he?"

"I've fixed him a soft bed."

"But I want to see him."

"Not yet."

It was then that the tears came. Virginia wasn't sure if the small girl was crying because she was worried about Murphy or because she couldn't see him immediately as she wanted. Jonathan just held her and let her weep. Virginia knew they all would be thankful when this ordeal was over.

————

A long, slow road back for Murphy eventually resulted in a nearly-good-as-new dog. The hair grew back to cover his scar, and he finally was running about the yard again, though he always had a bit of a limp. He played with Mindy as energetically as ever, even with the metal pin that held his shoulder together, but he did not go back into the horse corrals. He would bark at the animals through the rails—from a safe distance.

———

Virginia was busier than ever putting up summer garden produce. Grandmother Withers provided an extra pair of hands and many years of experience. They sat hour after hour at the kitchen table preparing vegetables or fruit for the cooking pot or canning jars, chatting as they worked. Soon the shelves in the cellar were filling up with shining jars of fruit and vegetables that would get them through the winter months.

Virginia went to bed weary but satisfied. The nights never seemed long enough. In a few short hours there would be breakfast to fix for hungry tummies, the usual housekeeping chores, and more canning.

Martha was now pulling herself up and walking around furniture. She had to be watched every minute to make sure she wouldn't grab a hot pot or reach out to the stove. She loved nothing better than to climb, and the stairs attracted her like a magnet. Virginia had to construct a barrier so the child couldn't get to them.

Mindy helped keep an eye on her and screamed for Virginia if she thought the baby was in danger. Virginia appreciated the warnings but not the screeches. She tried to tell Mindy to call softly and she would come, but Mindy always seemed to panic when the baby neared what she considered to be a danger zone. Her sudden squeal often startled both Virginia and Grandmother Withers.

"This is when one could appreciate one of those fancy new hearing pieces," Grandmother Withers remarked wryly. "Then you could turn it off."

Virginia agreed as she went to rescue Martha from her precarious perch on the plant stand. Only one violet was upside-down on the floor.

Virginia's tasks slackened as the growing season drew to a close. She could not help but breathe a sigh of relief. Perhaps she would have the chance to catch her breath. She looked forward to long winter evenings when she and Grandmother could sit around the quilting frames, stitching and chatting. Or perhaps they could fashion some new rag rugs. The one at the back door was looking rather faded from its many washings.

At any rate, it would be good to be able to sit for a while instead of rushing about from early dawn until dusk. She broached the subject with Grandmother as they cleared up the breakfast dishes.

"Frost on the ground last night," Virginia said. "Winter is coming. Like old Mr. Adamson used to say, 'I can smell it in the air.' I've been doing some thinking. It's about time to lay in supplies for winter's handwork. What would you like to start with? Jonathan said he'd be going into town today. I thought one of us might ride along and pick up some material."

Grandmother Withers hesitated for a few moments before answering. She placed the spoons she had just dried in the kitchen drawer and pushed it shut. "I've noticed the cold coming on too. It seems that our autumn is nearly spent."

"Do you want to go in with Jonathan, or shall I?" asked Virginia. "We could all go, for that matter. It would be fun to have a trip into town. Who knows when we might get another chance if we get a good storm that closes the roads." She pulled at her apron strings.

"I was rather thinking that I would go."

"Let's all go. The girls would enjoy the ride. What shall we shop for? Quilting material or something else?

What would you like to do to start out the winter? You choose."

Again Grandmother hesitated. "I . . . I should prune back that rose by the door."

Virginia was puzzled. "Jonathan is about ready to go. We should get our coats and bundle up the girls. You can do the rose when we get back."

"Virginia, I won't be coming back."

Virginia spun around, her apron hanging limply in her hands. "Whatever do you mean?"

"I'm thinking it's about time I got acquainted with those folks at the boardinghouse."

"But you can't. It's . . . it's unthinkable."

"It was my plan all along. You know that, dear. I've already got my bags packed."

CHAPTER 19

*J*onathan, too, protested. "There's no need for you to move to the boardinghouse," he told Grandmother Withers. "We love having you here with us."

"You deserve to be alone—as a family. Do you realize that in the two and a half years you've been married, I have lived with you for fully half that time?"

Virginia had not realized, but she had not been counting.

"It's time for you to have your own home to yourselves. I will be just fine in town. It will give me a chance to visit with some old friends."

Virginia wondered to whom Grandmother Withers was referring. She had made few friends in the little town. She had been there a relatively short time and had been busy with her flowers and taking care of Jonathan.

"Mrs. Cadbury has promised to come to tea once a week," she elaborated.

"They have facilities there for you to serve tea?" Virginia asked.

Grandmother Withers backtracked. "Well . . . I'm not sure yet. But if they don't, I'll walk on over to Mrs. Cadbury's. The exercise would do me good."

Virginia thought of the still-weak leg. It would be difficult for Grandmother Withers to walk the several blocks to Mrs. Cadbury's house.

When Jonathan determined that her mind was quite made up, he reluctantly loaded the bags.

"I will take you, Grandmother, because it is your wish. But remember, if you ever change your mind—today, tomorrow, or ten years from now—you are to come back. Promise me you'll not hesitate. You know you would be welcome."

She looked a bit teary eyed as she nodded solemnly.

They discovered that there would be no serving of tea to guests at the boardinghouse. Mrs. Withers was shown one very small room that enclosed a closet, a dresser, a bed, and one rather rickety-looking straight-backed chair. Two faded rag rugs were scattered on the floor. One equally faded picture, a stag leaping over a log in the middle of some forest, graced one wall. The wallpaper was old and yellowed, and the curtain at the one window hung limply.

Jonathan shook his head and was turning to carry the suitcases back to the car, but Grandmother Withers stopped him with her hand on his arm. "I'm staying" was all she said, but her eyes showed her determination.

Wordlessly he placed the two leather bags on the floor.

"They have a common room," the elderly woman hurried to explain. "One does not have to spend the entire time in the bedroom. They sit and chat and even play games—like checkers and things—out there. And they do serve tea—to the boarders—every afternoon."

She seemed to think that would console her grandson and his wife. But Virginia did not feel much better.

"I will miss the little ones," Grandmother admitted. "They've been such a blessing, and they grow so quickly."

Virginia felt a sadness fill her entire being. She had been so looking forward to leisurely winter evenings of fireside chats and handwork. Now it seemed she would be doing it all alone. She promised herself that, as long as the weather permitted, she would go in once a week for a visit with the elderly lady. She could pick her up and together they could go for tea to her mother's or Clara's. And of course they would stop to pick her up each Sunday and take her to church. With two visits per week they would stay in close touch. Grandmother wouldn't need to miss contact with the children.

But it wouldn't be the same. Not the same at all.

Even though Virginia had known she would miss Grandmother Withers, she had not realized how intense the feeling would be. Jonathan was always out, busy with the horses. Virginia realized, now that Grandmother was gone, that having the adult companionship had eased the loneliness from many hours. The chatter of small children didn't replace conversation with someone who shared one's life.

It was in this state that Virginia took on the weaning of her first child. She was not sure who endured the most—Martha or the small child's mama. Martha had no desire to drink from a cup and showed her displeasure at breakfast one morning when she knocked the cup from Jonathan's hand, sending milk flying across the floor and up the wall. Jonathan scolded and Martha howled and soon Mindy had joined in. In the midst of the uproar, Virginia knelt down and wiped up the mess.

In the early days of the weaning process, she felt a good deal of discomfort. The cold compresses advised did not seem to help much. Virginia was miserable. And Martha, who previously had dropped off for her afternoon nap with no difficulty, now lay in her crib and screamed. They all lived through the same chaos at bedtime. At times Virginia had to slip away from the house and let Jonathan bear the brunt of the bedtime trauma.

Mindy put her hands over her ears and cried along with Martha. Virginia feared that she might start wetting her bed again, but thankfully that did not happen.

It seemed to go on forever, but by the end of ten days Martha must have concluded that crying was not solving her problem. She gave in and fell asleep without the tantrum, and Mindy took her hands from her ears and did likewise.

Virginia, too, had weathered the storm. She could retire in comfort and arise rested the next morning. She was so glad to have it over. The infant milestone had proven to be more of a challenge than she had anticipated.

Mindy was the one who finally convinced Martha to use the cup. "Look, Martha. Look how I drink my milk. You want some?" And Mindy shared her cup with Martha, who seemed to think everything her older sister did was just about right.

"Do you want your own cup?" Mindy asked. And Martha did. From then on, every time Mindy lifted her cup for a sip, Martha did likewise.

But even with that ordeal over, Virginia still missed Grandmother Withers more than she would have thought possible. Could she pray that the woman would soon be back?

———

"Francine has a beau," announced Clara as they enjoyed some time in quiet. The cousins had been given their milk and cookies and sent off to play. Virginia smiled. It seemed that Francine had been entertaining beaus since she was in pigtails.

"Who this time?"

"No . . . I think this one might be serious. Honest."

Virginia's interest was piqued.

"She met him at the post office."

"Really?"

Francine had been hired to take over Virginia's job when they had moved out to the farm.

"You sound surprised," said Clara.

"Well, I am . . . I guess. I thought she would already know anyone who would come into the post office. I mean, she's lived here all her life. Grown up here."

"This fellow is new."

Virginia sipped her tea. "Tell me about him."

"Well, he's not country folk, I can tell you that. Nor from poor folk, by the look of him. Don't know much about him yet. He's in real estate or something. Seems nice enough."

"Churchgoer?" asked Virginia.

"Oh yes. In fact I think he has more enthusiasm than Francine."

"Have you ever . . . wondered about Francine?" asked Virginia candidly.

"In what way?"

"Well . . . remember how she was when she was little? So sensitive she'd cry over anything? It used to aggravate me something awful. She worried and fretted over everyone else's troubles—or imagined troubles."

Clara nodded. "She was always very tender."

"I don't know if I'd call it tender. I felt at times that she was . . . was manipulative . . . with her tears."

"Oh, I don't know. Of course, you were closer in age. I had already gone through my days of teenage trials by the time Francine was old enough to be a pest. You likely noticed it more."

Virginia nodded. Maybe that was so.

"Anyway, you were commenting on something about Francine."

"Well . . ." began Virginia, "she seemed to change. Right about the time she hit the teen years. She . . . she certainly doesn't fret over other people's problems anymore."

"No."

"Sometimes I'm afraid that the only person who really interests her at all is Francine."

"You think she's grown selfish?"

"I was thinking more . . . self-centered."

"Oh, I think you are being a bit harsh. She's still just . . . just a child, really."

"Clara, you were married, with a child, by her age."

Clara looked surprised, then smiled and nodded.

"And if this new beau is . . . citified, well-to-do, then I worry about it. Is that what has attracted her to him?"

"I don't know, but he seems plenty attracted to her as well. She hasn't just thrown herself at him."

"She didn't need to throw herself at any of them. She's beautiful. She's charming. Every fellow for miles around has been throwing himself at her. It's gone on for years."

"I suppose it could go to a girl's head. I wouldn't know. For me there was only Troy."

Virginia was silent. She stared at the cup in her hands.

"Well, I say we give them both the benefit of doubt," commented Clara. "Let them prove what they're made of. If this is just another feather in Francine's cap, so to speak, she'll soon forget him."

"But if he's a nice young man, as you seem to think, is it fair to him?"

Clara had no answer.

The winter settled around them with a vengeance. There were a number of weeks when Virginia did not get to town midweek. They missed some Sunday services. They were even snowbound over Christmas, so their plans to fetch Grandmother Withers to the farm were canceled in much disappointment.

Virginia still longed for the woman's cheery companionship. Her wise comments. Her smile on the children as they performed their little antics or pushed up against her knee.

I wish she wouldn't be so stubborn, Virginia found herself thinking on more than one occasion. But then she would tell herself if Grandmother Withers preferred to be on her own, that was within her right.

Following an unusual early March storm, Jonathan decided he needed to make a trip into town despite the road conditions. Virginia stayed behind, knowing it was not wise to attempt the trip with the children. Jonathan likely would spend much of his time shoveling the motorcar through snowdrifts.

When Jonathan returned some hours later, he had Grandmother Withers with him, bundled in blankets and tucked in the back seat.

"She's been ill for days," explained Jonathan, his voice low. "Too weak to even get out of bed."

Virginia did not have words to express her concern. Her eyes filled with tears at the sight of the wasted woman. "Oh, Grandmother."

They got her into the warmth of the house, and Jonathan brought her bed down from the upstairs room. After she had been tucked in and made as comfortable as possible, Dr. Luke paid a visit. He brought medication to help relieve the congestion, suggested steaming and chicken broth, and left shaking his head.

Virginia's time now was filled with being the nurse. Her mother's nursing abilities had not come her way, and she knew little about caring for the sick. But she fussed and comforted and gave back rubs and sponge baths. The children seemed to understand the seriousness of the situation and, for the most part, played quietly together.

Gradually, with the passing of time and the care and medication, the fever broke and the coughing decreased. Virginia sighed with relief.

"We don't want you to go back to the boardinghouse," Virginia said firmly one day. "Jonathan has been into town and removed all your personal things from the room and settled your account. Everything is ready upstairs in your bedroom. Please, Grandmother, don't argue with us about this. We want you here. We need you here."

The elderly woman reached up a shaky hand to touch Virginia's cheek.

"I missed you all so much" was all she said, but Virginia knew that the matter was settled.

———

Greeting the spring season once again meant muddy tracks and muck-covered overalls as the corrals went through the usual thawing out time. But as an offset to the mess, Virginia also watched for early buds and blossoms. And when the first robin called outside the kitchen window, she felt spring was truly ready to release them from the grip of winter.

Her heart was ready to have its burden lifted. With

spring, surely Grandmother Withers would get some
strength back. Surely life could take up where it had left
off the summer before. There would be the flowers, the
garden of vegetables, the warm days spent on the porch
shelling peas or cutting rhubarb. Life would be better now.

And with each day there was slow improvement. But
Virginia soon realized that things would never again go
back to being the same with her beloved companion.
Grandmother Withers did not have the strength to enjoy
digging in the flower beds or pulling weeds from rows of
young carrots. She hardly had strength to walk to the
porch to sit in the sun.

But she still was wonderful company. Her cheerful
greeting and her broad smile helped to brighten the day
for each family member. Martha joined Mindy in the
story times. And Grandmother managed to entertain the
two little ones for hours of the day while Virginia hurried
from one task to another.

"I think Grandmother needs her stick back," Mindy
observed, and amid chuckles the cane was put back into
use. Mindy had to have hers back as well, and of course
Jonathan had to fashion one for little Martha. All day long
Virginia listened to the *thump, thump* of walking sticks as
the three moved about the house. Martha did not understand that her cane was to move in unison with her step,
so she just pounded it on the floor as she went, a happy
grin on her little round face. It could have been irritating
had Virginia not reminded herself of the reason for the
thumps. She only smiled and went on peeling potatoes for
supper or mincing onions for the stew. At least they were
together. For that she was very thankful.

In spite of her busy summer, Virginia felt happy. With
the warmer, dryer weather, the children were able to spend
much of their time outside romping in the sun's warm
rays. Murphy watched over them, limping along with

them wherever they went. Virginia had to laugh one day as she came in from the garden with a mess of fresh beans and saw tiny Martha trying to offer Murphy a walking stick. Murphy looked patient but totally perplexed as the youngster kept trying to shove the stick in his paw. "He'yah, Mu'fy," she told him over and over.

Virginia shared the story with Grandmother Withers and later again with Jonathan when he came in at the end of the day.

"Well, I guess she thinks it works for limps" was Jonathan's comment. And they all laughed again.

CHAPTER 20

"There's a letter from my mother," Jonathan said as he set Virginia's grocery order from town on the table beside her.

Virginia wiped her hands on a nearby kitchen towel. "What did she say?"

"It was addressed to both of us." Jonathan never opened mail that was sent to them both until they were together. Virginia nodded toward the envelope that lay beside the groceries and said simply, "Please read it to me."

Jonathan did not scan the letter first but began at once to read it aloud. Her mother-in-law was planning a visit from their ranch in the West. She wanted to see Jonathan's Mindy and the new baby daughter. She also wanted to see her mother. It had been a long time.

"When is she coming?" asked Virginia, her voice holding both anticipation and concern. Her eyes automatically traveled around the room, noting things she would want to attend to before the visit.

"The end of the month—if it's all right with us. It is, isn't it?"

"Of course," responded Virginia. "It will be wonderful to have her come. Grandmother will be so glad to see her."

"The 'baby,'" chuckled Jonathan as he reread portions of the letter. "She'll be some surprised if she expects to find a baby. Martha's out there right now trying to dig a hole for Murphy to hide in."

"Oh, she's not! Where?"

"In that south flower bed," said Jonathan with a grin. "The dirt's nice and soft there."

Virginia hurried from the kitchen, hopeful she would be in time to rescue her plants and keep Martha from making a total mess of herself and the yard.

Jonathan was right. There was Martha, big kitchen spoon in hand, dirt flying in every direction.

"Martha! Stop it!" Virginia called before even reaching the child.

Martha pushed up on chubby legs to her full height of twenty-nine inches. "Mu'fy," she said, pointing to the hole she had dug, eyes shining with glee.

"Murphy does not need a hole," Virginia remonstrated as she began to brush the child off. "And where on earth did you get my spoon?"

"In there," said Martha pointing toward the house.

Virginia pushed dirt back into the hole with one foot, picked up Martha and the spoon, and headed back to the kitchen.

"There's a P.S.," said Jonathan as Virginia entered the room. "I didn't notice it before."

Virginia plopped Martha on the floor, took the spoon from her hand, and straightened, her eyes on Jonathan.

"She says she plans to bring Slate with her."

"A slate? Why? How will she manage that? And what does she want to do with it when she gets it here?"

Jonathan laughed heartily. "Well, I can sure enough understand your confusion there," he said. "Always said it was a strange name for a boy."

"A boy?"

"My oldest sister's son. She called him Slate. Don't ask me why, but it's rather a common name out in those parts."

"So your mother is bringing a child with her?" asked Virginia returning to his first statement.

"Yeah. That's what she says here. She plans on bringing Slate with her, if it's all right. She says he can't wait to see the place. Thinks I'm the luckiest guy in the world to be working with horses."

But Virginia's head already was spinning with plans and questions. Her mother-in-law could use the guest room where Grandmother Withers had been before she was taken ill, but where would she put another child? The upstairs had three bedrooms, and Grandmother Withers was still occupying the living room.

The living room, Virginia's thoughts rushed on. What would Jonathan's mother think of the living room? They could scarcely turn around in there. And the walls still were raw plaster. Jonathan had not found time to put on a coat of paint.

Oh dear, thought Virginia. *The end of the month is only two weeks away*. How would she ever be ready to greet her mother-in-law?

She looked quickly around her kitchen. Its walls still needed color, and the cupboards had not yet been stained. The curtains were up "temporarily," and the floor was waiting for its covering. But it was clean and it had been serviceable and roomy. Almost comfy. But with her mother-in-law coming?

Virginia's mind was not totally on the supper preparations that evening.

———

There didn't seem to be very much Virginia could do over the next two weeks to improve her house. She did clean it thoroughly from top to bottom, even though Jonathan insisted that it didn't need it. But there was no way to make more space in the living room. And she did not want to make Grandmother Withers feel that her bed in there was an imposition. Virginia concentrated instead on the kitchen and the guest room upstairs. She scrubbed the cupboards and table until they glistened. She washed the windows and the curtains, starching the latter so stiff they scarcely dared hang in folds. She polished the stove until the enamel and chrome reflected her face.

The bedroom got the same careful attention. The latest quilt, as yet not used, graced the four-poster Jonathan had purchased at the local hardware store. A new braided rug covered the area in front of the bed. The curtains were crisp and clean at the room's one window, and the small chest brought from her girlhood bedroom stood against one wall, a gold-rimmed blue pitcher and bowl sitting proudly on its surface. Still Virginia worried. The room looked so small, so bare. . . .

I'll bring up one of the chairs from the living room, she decided. Which she did, draping a knitted afghan over the back. She felt that it looked much better. And it also helped to add a bit more space to the living room below.

Now, what about the little boy? Where will he sleep? she wondered frantically. But when she brought up the subject with Jonathan, he dismissed her concerns with a wave of his hand! "Oh, we'll find some place to tuck him in," he said airily.

Virginia turned her attention to baking. At least she should have something to serve her special guests.

Virginia could not still the butterflies as they waited for the incoming train. Grandmother Withers had announced that she would wait at home, no doubt aware that the motorcar would not hold all of them.

"You go and let me stay," Virginia had urged, but the older woman had insisted that a trip to town was more than she cared to exert herself for. She preferred the peace and comfort of her own rocking chair. So Jonathan and Virginia, with the two children brushed and polished to perfection, were now on the platform to meet the incoming train. Virginia's nervous stomach churned right along with its rolling wheels.

She had enjoyed meeting Damaris Lewis years before, but the woman had not been her mother-in-law then. Virginia had felt no need to live up to any expectations. But things were quite different now. Virginia did hope that she wouldn't let Jonathan down. That his mother might approve of the choice he had made. That she might be proud of her grandchildren.

Virginia watched the travelers disembark. For a fleeting moment she thought perhaps their guests had missed their train or changed their plans. It seemed that all the passengers had already alighted. Then a tall young man carrying two heavy cases descended the steps of the railway car. He was followed closely by a woman wrapped in a fashionable traveling coat, a matching hat almost hiding her face. Jonathan moved forward, and Virginia knew that her mother-in-law was here.

But she did not step forward herself. This moment belonged to Jonathan. There would be time for her to greet their guests soon enough.

Jonathan wrapped his arms around his mother's shoulders. She hugged him for what seemed to be a very long time. Virginia didn't hear any words exchanged, but perhaps they needed none. When the embrace ended, the woman dabbed at her eyes and Jonathan turned his attention to the young man who stood silently to the side.

"Slate," Virginia heard him say. "You've grown outa your breeches, boy."

The boy grinned as he shook Jonathan's hand; then they, too, embraced.

Slate? thought Virginia. *They said she was bringing a child. This is Slate?*

Jonathan placed one arm around each of the newcomers and steered them toward Virginia and the children. "You've met Virginia, Mother."

"Yes," said the woman with an open smile and open arms. "It's so good to see you again, Virginia, dear. Mother writes such wonderful things about you."

Virginia felt her face flush. She hadn't realized that Grandmother Withers was sending written reports.

"And the children. How she loves the children," enthused Damaris.

The children. Virginia had almost forgotten they were with her. She felt Mindy lean up against her now. Virginia reached down a hand, thankful to have her close.

"This is our Mindy," Jonathan was saying, and Mindy, with typical shyness, pressed closer against Virginia.

"And Martha . . ." he began. "Where is Martha?"

Virginia whirled around. *Where is Martha?*

But there she was, not four feet away, in her favorite squatting position, her clean frock streaked with some kind of platform grime, her neatly tied hair ribbon askew in her curls. She looked up just as the group looked her

226

way and gave them one of her impish grins. Protruding from her mouth at a rakish angle was someone's discarded cigarette butt.

―――――――

It was obvious from the very first day that Jonathan's love of horses was equaled by that of young Slate. "Boy, I've never seen such horses," he said over and over, his eyes glowing with admiration.

Virginia could tell that the open praise was not lost on his uncle Jonathan. "You want to handle them some?" he suggested.

It was a question that did not need an answer.

She watched as the two went to the barns and the corrals. Slate looked on as Jonathan put some of the younger stock through their paces. Then Jonathan passed him the training rein.

With a bit of coaching he soon was handling it well. He seemed to be a natural in working with the animals. Virginia knew that he'd had experience on his father's ranch, but she had not expected to see a boy of sixteen— which was Slate's age—handling high-spirited horses with such obvious ease.

"He's got the right touch," Jonathan said to her proudly as he prepared for bed. "Soft hands. Horses know that. They also sense fear. There is no fear in that boy. He'd have gone out there and worked with the stallions if I'd let him."

"I saw that. Even I could tell," answered Virginia.

"How did your day go?"

She smiled. "Your mother is very sweet, Jonathan. She is still chuckling over her first glimpse of Martha. And she's been so nice about the house—how we are all crowded into the living room and all. She didn't even seem to notice when I sent Slate up to get the chair from her room. I forgot we'd need it in the living room while she's here. We'll have to get us a chair for the bedroom as soon as we're able. It's not right for a guest to have no place to sit and unlace her shoes."

"I knew she'd love you," said Jonathan, drawing Virginia close and kissing her forehead. "My mother and I have the same faultless good taste."

Virginia snuggled up against him. "I like young Slate too. Did you notice him with the children? Even Mindy has warmed up to him, and Martha—she follows him around like a puppy."

"He's used to little ones, being the oldest of five."

"And it was so nice of him to offer to sleep in the loft."

Jonathan laughed softly. "Well, it wasn't exactly niceness—I can tell you that right now. He was aching for a chance to move in with those horses. No, sir, that was no hardship for the boy."

"Well, it was nice of him all the same," insisted Virginia.

"I'm so glad Mother came," said Jonathan in a more serious tone. "I don't think Grandmother is doing all that well. Mother never would forgive herself if anything happened before she could see her again."

His whispered words struck fear to Virginia's heart. Surely Jonathan did not think that . . . that Grandmother Withers was in danger. True, she did not seem to be gaining strength. But there had been some improvement, and as the weeks passed there would be more . . . wouldn't there?

"You don't think she's getting better?" asked Virginia, her voice tight.

Jonathan's arms pulled her closer. "She's much better than she was," he said carefully. "With all your good nursing . . . she's much better."

"But. . . ?" prompted Virginia.

"Luke says she has a poor heart. There's nothing he can do about it. We just have to keep her with us. Let her enjoy the children. Try to keep her out of drafts so she doesn't catch another of those vicious colds. And pray for the best for her. That's about all we can do."

Virginia was silent for a long time.

"Why didn't you tell me?" she finally ventured.

He was slow to answer. "I guess I . . . didn't figure there was anything to be gained by it. I knew you'd worry. And maybe . . . maybe I thought if I didn't acknowledge it, it would go away. I dunno. Guess I've been hoping Luke was wrong."

"But you don't think he is?"

"No. No, I guess not. Not anymore. Last time he checked, he said she's getting worse."

Virginia had no words. Thoughts and feeling and fears swirled around inside her. She couldn't bear to think of life without Grandmother Withers.

"Does your mother know?" she heard her own trembling voice asking.

"It's not the kind of thing I could write in a letter."

"Are you going to tell her now?"

She heard him swallow. Once. Twice. "I guess I'll have to."

Virginia laid her head against his chest and tried to think clearly. To absorb what she had just heard. Surely it wasn't true. Surely not. How could she ever get along without Grandmother? What would the loss do to the children? To Mindy especially? Who would read them stories, kiss bumps and bruises all better? Sing them silly songs that made them giggle? It was too much. She would simply refuse to think about it.

But even as she fought to push the knowledge to the

back of her mind, the reality of what they might be facing overwhelmed her. Hot tears washed down her cheeks and dampened Jonathan's nightshirt even as she felt his arms tightening about her.

CHAPTER 21

*O*n a summer's day promising to smother them with stifling heat, a grim-faced Mr. Woods climbed from the motorcar in their driveway. Virginia met him at the door. The expression on his face made Virginia think this was no casual neighborly call or grandfatherly visit. She did not ask his mission but waited anxiously for him to explain. With all her heart she hoped it was not bad news about Jenny.

"Jenny called" were his first words, and Virginia released the breath she had been holding. At least Jenny was alive.

"Hayden has been killed in a motor accident."

Virginia's hand went to her throat.

"She wondered if you could come."

Virginia's head was spinning. How could she go to Jenny? She was a wife and mother. She had an ailing grandmother in her home who needed her care. She had houseguests.

"I'm going down on the afternoon train. I'd be glad to have you travel with me."

Still Virginia had not spoken. She finally nodded dumbly and managed, "I'm so sorry."

He nodded in return.

"I'll be at the station," he said. "If you can't make it, I understand. Jenny just wanted me to ask, and I . . . I didn't want to let her down."

She nodded again, and he turned and went back to his car.

The adults of the household were soon gathered to discuss the news.

"Do you want to go?" asked Jonathan, who had come in from the barn when he saw the car.

Virginia shook her head, then changed to a nod. "I don't know," she said, brushing back strands of hair with an agitated hand. "I . . . I'd rather do just about anything else . . . but she sent for me. I've been trying all these years to . . . to get through to her. Is this the time? I don't know. But how. . . ?" She didn't finish the thought.

"I think you should go," said Damaris softly. "I know it won't be easy, but you seem to be her only link with anything solid and true. Anything good. It sounds like she needs you now."

"But the children. Grandmother. I . . ."

"I can look after things here. I'm sure Jonathan can help me learn what to do and where things are."

Jonathan doesn't know where things are either, Virginia could have said but didn't.

"I think you should go too," Jonathan said quickly. "I might not be much help here, but Grandmother can advise. She knows how you've run the house and cared for the girls. Between us, we'll manage."

Virginia packed a small bag, kissed her little ones a tearful good-bye, and was driven to town by Jonathan to catch the late afternoon train. "I'll be praying for you . . . and for Jenny," he whispered into her ear as he hugged her at the depot.

It was a long and silent journey. Neither she nor Mr. Woods were much inclined to talk. Virginia wondered if he was dreading the coming meeting with Jenny as much as she was.

When they arrived in the city, they made their way through the train station and down the wide front steps. Mr. Woods hailed a cab and handed the driver the slip of paper on which he'd written the address Jenny had given him.

They wound their way in and out of traffic and through the strange streets. Virginia thought about her previous visit to the city and wondered if Pastor Black still shepherded the little congregation. He and his mother had been very good to her when she had been on another rescue effort for Jenny.

At last they arrived at a large building. They stared up at it while the driver insisted it was where they wanted to be. "The address says it's up the steps. Third floor," he said gruffly as he took the bills from Mr. Woods and handed back the address.

They went in together. The place smelled like meals from many yesterdays mixed with smoke-stale draperies and musty carpets. The elevator smelled even worse. They decided to take the stairs.

By the time she had climbed to the third floor, Virginia felt a little sick to her stomach. She didn't know if it was nerves, dreading what lay ahead, hunger from not having eaten properly, or nausea from all the odors they had encountered.

Mr. Woods found the door marked with a faint *307* and knocked. At first there was no response. He knocked again. More loudly. A voice from somewhere inside said, "Who is it?"

Mr. Woods responded, giving Virginia's name as well as his own.

"Just a minute," came the slurred voice again. There was a stirring about, a door chain being unhooked, and then the door opened. There was Jenny. It was all Virginia could do to keep from gasping.

Jenny, as Virginia had never seen her before. Jenny, clothed in a ragged robe, her hair entangled about a pale, ghostlike face, eyes red and swollen. Jenny, smelling of alcohol and stale cigarette smoke.

"You came," Jenny rasped out, and her face crumpled. She threw herself in Virginia's arms and sobbed uncontrollably.

Mr. Woods rescued Virginia's small valise and managed somehow to maneuver them both inside so he could shut the door. It was some minutes before Jenny was in control enough to converse.

With a great many sobs and pauses, Jenny told them that Hayden and his new wife had been out with friends. Coming home in the early morning hours, the driver had missed a curve or fallen asleep. No one knew for sure. The car had lurched down an embankment. The new Mrs. Hayden had been thrown clear. She and another passenger were injured only slightly and had already been released from hospital. Another of Hayden's friends had also been killed. The two had been pinned under the car when it rolled. The driver was in the hospital in serious condition.

By the time Jenny had choked out the details, it was

late. The one-room apartment had only one bed. Mr. Woods said that he would take a hotel and be back in the morning. Virginia envied him. She had the feeling she was in for a very long night.

After the door had closed upon her father, Jenny poured herself another drink. Virginia sat rigid in the room's one chair. She had never been in such a situation before. The room, obviously the place Jenny called home, was dark and dirty and sparsely furnished with old, worn pieces. Jenny's clothing, bottles, magazines, and old newspapers cluttered the room. The whole place smelled even worse than the stairway they had climbed.

Jenny looked up from the drink in her hand. "What's the matter, Virginia?" she asked, her words slurred. "You surprised that the town's alcoholic newsman has produced an alcoholic daughter?"

Virginia wanted to respond that the town newsman was an alcoholic no longer, but she held her tongue.

"I hope you didn't come all this way to lecture me on making choices," Jenny continued. " 'Cause I've no mind to be listening to your little Sunday school talks on the goodness of God."

Virginia shook her head. "I did not come to lecture you, Jenny. You know that."

"Good." Jenny burped, then giggled. It sounded silly and out of place under such circumstances. Virginia cringed, realizing that Jenny was indeed intoxicated.

Jenny flopped down onto an open space on the floor and crossed her legs in a most unladylike fashion, her dirty robe unable to cover her properly.

"I'll bet you're thinkin', 'Good riddance.' " Jenny swore. " 'He's gone. Now maybe Jenny will stop chasing after someone she can't have and clean up her life.' Is that what you think, Virginia? Well, it won't work. I like my life just fine. At least I used to."

She took another gulp from the glass in her hand.

"Virginia, do you have any idea what it's like to be the 'ex'? No, of course you don't. You've never been the 'ex.' Except for the ex-girlfriend of one sharp guy—Jamison whatever his name was. Well, I'll tell you what it's like to be the 'ex.' Ex-wife. Tomorrow the man I love is going to be buried. Tomorrow I won't even be given a place to sit at the ceremony." She interrupted herself, one hand raising her glass. "Do you call it a ceremony when you bury someone, or is that just weddings and baptisms and such? Anyway, they'll be burying the one I love—have always loved. I'll be there—you can count on it—but I won't be welcomed. They'd lock me out if they could. They didn't even have the decency to tell me he died. No—I had to read it in the papers. Read it. Right there. I wasn't even mentioned in the obituary. Read it!" she demanded, pointing at one of the papers scattered on the floor. She began to sob again.

"Did anyone ask me where he should be buried?" she rasped out when she could go on. "What should be written on the gravestone? I don't matter, you see. I'm just the 'ex.' It's like I never lived. Never had his child. Like I don't exist anymore. They wouldn't even let me in to see his body. They locked me out." Again she put a shaking hand to her face and sobbed wildly.

"Well, they won't lock me out of that church. Paper says right there where he's . . . where that service takes place. I'll be there. Hayden would want me there. Sure, we had our differences . . . but he would want me there. That . . ." Jenny then used unspeakable language to describe Hayden's widow. "She can't keep me away. That's *my* Hayden they'll be burying."

"Jenny, I think you should try to get some sleep. Tomorrow is going to be a difficult day. You need your rest," Virginia said gently.

"Sleep?" Jenny scoffed. "How can I sleep? This is the last night before Hayden is put in the ground. Tomorrow . . . he will be gone. Gone, Virginia. Don't you understand? Gone. Forever. My Hayden." Her words were becoming louder, more slurred.

Yes, mourned Virginia. *I do understand. The helplessness, the hopelessness, of those who die without knowing God, without a Saviour. No wonder you weep, Jenny. No wonder you try to numb your pain with alcohol.*

Jenny swiped at clutter on the floor to clear herself a larger space. She lay down, spilling her drink on the already stained carpet. "Pour me another one, Virginia," she said, lifting up her glass.

"I'm sorry, I can't do that," said Virginia, rising from her chair. "If you have to have another one, you'll have to get it yourself."

Virginia crossed to the area that seemed to serve as Jenny's kitchen. "Have you had anything to eat?"

For a moment Jenny looked puzzled. "I dunno," she said at last. "I think so. I dunno."

"You should eat."

"Why don't you fix me roast beef and mashed potatoes?" said Jenny, then broke into riotous laugher, rolling on the floor. Virginia had never seen such erratic behavior. One minute weeping uncontrollably, the next minute laughing hilariously. It was truly frightening.

"Tell you what, good neighbor," Jenny went on. "If you find it, you can fix it." She laughed again and scrambled unsteadily to her feet to retrieve her bottle.

Jenny was right. As Virginia sorted through the clutter, she found nothing fit to eat.

"I think you should get to bed," she said again, but Jenny was bending over, holding on to her stomach.

"I feel a little sick. I think . . . ." She headed for the corner of the room where an open door displayed a stained sink and toilet. But Jenny never made it that far. She was sick in the middle of the floor. Virginia found it difficult to keep from heaving herself.

She helped Jenny to the bed and found a pail and some rags by the sink. She could not do a thorough job of the cleanup, but at least there was some improvement. Some clutter on the floor had also been soiled. Virginia did not know how to clean it or what to do with it. She wished she could just bag it up and throw it out.

There was no way that she could get rid of the putrid odor. It hung in the room, saturating the very air she had to breathe. She went to the room's one window in the hope of getting some fresh air, but it would not open.

By the time she turned around, Jenny was already in a deep sleep. Virginia looked about her, hot tears washing down her face. *Oh, Jenny*, her heart cried. *What has happened to you?* And Virginia wept for her childhood friend as she never had before.

————

Mr. Woods took them both out for breakfast, and then Virginia went back to the apartment to do a more thorough cleaning while father and daughter went off somewhere on their own. When they returned, Jenny was wearing a new black suit and her hair had been properly tamed and tucked under a matching hat. She looked a little more like the Jenny of old. How he had managed to keep Jenny from the bottle, Virginia never knew.

The three went to the service together by cab to the old-style stone church. They slipped into a back-row pew and sat stiffly while the organ played. Virginia thought she was able to pick out Hayden's current widow in a group of young adults toward the front. Old before their time, their faces were ravaged by hard living and by the despair of death with no hope.

The service was short and dismal. The minister did make reference to "the dear departed, who has ended his earthly journey and is now enjoying the rewards of that unknown land." It left Virginia feeling cold and hopeless. She wondered if Jenny—sitting beside her in stony silence—was feeling the same way.

She was thankful to leave the dimness of the building and get out into the fresh air. But what would happen to Jenny now?

———

Mr. Woods tried to talk Jenny into going home with him, but she refused. He was hesitant to leave her in her present condition and her obvious dependence on drink. Virginia supposed he would understand better than anyone else. Realizing that there was little he could do, he reluctantly left.

"I have to get home, Jenny," Virginia told her two days later. "You understand."

Jenny nodded. "I know. I know—you've got kids."

Jenny had not even asked about Mindy.

"Yes. And Grandmother Withers is not well. We have her with us."

Jenny did not answer.

"Why don't you come back with me?" Virginia offered. "It would be good for you to get away for a while."

But Jenny shook her head. "There's nothing to go back to."

"Is there anything to stay here for?"

Jenny sighed. "Maybe not. Maybe there's nothing to live for at all."

Her words frightened Virginia. She knelt before Jenny, taking her hand in her own. "Jenny, listen, please. We love you. Your father and I both love you. We'd . . . we'd help you if you'd let us. If there was any way at all . . ."

To her surprise Jenny leaned forward and pulled Virginia's head up against her chest. "I know that, Virginia," she admitted, her voice choked with tears. "I know that. That's why I sent for you. You've been a good friend, Virginia. All these years when I've been a . . . a bad friend for you. And I love you for it, Virginia. Don't think I don't. But I . . . I'm not ready for a change yet. I have a lot of thinking to do. I can't face it yet."

Virginia held her close, then rose to her feet. The cab was waiting to take her to the train.

———

Virginia was so thankful to be home. It seemed like she had been gone forever. Her eyes moved from one to the other of those she loved dearest, thankful they were all there, whole and healthy. And each one of them welcomed her in a special way. Mindy pressed close and shadowed each step she took for the first half hour. Martha covered her with sloppy kisses, then busied herself with tugging the valise around the kitchen. Grandmother smiled her welcome from her chair by the fireplace. And Jonathan grinned when Virginia noticed the new trim round the main floor windows.

"Slate's been a big help with the horses. And Mother said it was about time I kept my promise to finish off the house. Long way to go yet, but it's a start."

There had been other subtle changes as well, even in the short time she had been gone. Mindy had opened up to her Grandmother Damaris. She followed her around the house chatting nonstop. Martha, on the other hand, had claimed Slate. He could not get through the door before she ran to him, insisting on being picked up and carried about. He seemed to accept it good-naturedly. Virginia wondered if he might even be a little flattered by all the attention from the child.

––––––

Murphy's frantic barking drew Virginia to the kitchen window. He was in the corrals, a place he had not been since his accident. Virginia watched as he stood, four paws planted firmly, challenging the approach of the stallion Warrior. Warrior was the one horse that Virginia feared. Though Jonathan was able to handle him, he advised everyone else to stay clear of Warrior's corral. The stallion was very protective of his territory and totally unpredictable. One never knew when he might decide to whirl and kick or bare his teeth and charge.

Now Murphy seemed about to reap the wrath of the snorting animal. *That foolish dog*, thought Virginia. *This time he will get his head kicked in for sure.*

But then Virginia saw Slate running toward the corrals. *Oh, I hope he doesn't go in there to protect that dog,* Virginia's thoughts hurried on. *Better to lose a dog than have the boy injured.*

It was then she spotted the patch of blue inside the corral fence. *Blue. Martha is wearing blue. Surely Martha . . .* Panic struck. Virginia whirled and raced from the house. Martha was out in that pen with that half-crazed stallion. It was not Murphy that Slate was running to save—it was Martha!

Even as she ran, Virginia saw Slate crawl over the rails and move slowly down on the other side. He approached the stallion cautiously, hand outstretched. *No, Slate. Get out of there*, Virginia wanted to scream, but she could not. They had to get Martha before the whirling, tramping hooves came down on her little body.

At the appearance of the boy, Murphy had wisely backed off. The horse now needed to be calmed rather than driven.

As Slate approached, the stallion tossed his head, mane whipping wildly over his arched neck. He snorted, reared and tossed his head again, and came down, pawing the ground.

But as Slate drew nearer Warrior backed a step. Then another step. Another. He was still blowing and snorting, white eyes wild. Virginia was frozen to the spot. Like Murphy, she knew that Warrior needed no other distraction. She put her hands to her mouth to prevent the scream that felt like it was choking her. Would Warrior charge? And if he did, would it be right over the hapless Martha?

But, no, as Slate moved forward, he was gradually— oh, so gradually—turning the horse aside. Virginia could hear the soft murmur of his voice now. He was coaxing, talking, charming the animal. But his words were not just for the stallion. Virginia heard the words, spoken in the very same tone of voice: "Go to the fence, Martha. That's a good girl. Get out of the corral. Good girl." And all of the time he was drawing closer and closer to the horse. Warrior was no longer backing away, though he still stomped and snorted. And Martha—bless her little heart—was crawling toward the corral fence, eyes big, blue dress dragging in the dirt. She was almost there. Almost.

Virginia knew she should not run forward and risk spooking the horse. Yet it was all she could do to hold her ground. Surely Martha would not turn around and go back to Slate. Surely not.

And then, miraculously, Slate was rubbing the stallion's nose. The horse flinched, muscles rippling in the morning sun. Slate's hand stole up warrior's neck, patting, massaging, while the animal stood as though uncertain what to do. Slate moved his head just enough to check on

Martha, gave the arched neck one more pat, and backed slowly away. Warrior snorted again, tossed his head and whirled around to race to the other end of the corral, head and tail held high.

Virginia dropped to the ground in a heap, hands to her face, tears flowing uncontrolled. The next thing she knew, Murphy was licking her face. She placed her arms around his neck and buried her fingers in his tangled coat. "You crazy old dog," she cried. "You crazy old lame dog."

And then Slate was placing Martha in her arms. *Slate.* He would always be someone very special in Virginia's eyes.

CHAPTER 22

$\mathcal{O}$ne did not travel halfway across a continent for only a short visit, so Virginia was quite prepared for her guests to be in her home for at least some weeks. For the most part they were good weeks for her. Damaris soon made her forget her concern about measuring up as a daughter-in-law, helping with meals and dishes and even garden work. The children loved their "new" grandma. The afternoon breaks for tea while Martha slept and Mindy watched the men work the horses were special, as the three ladies talked about their lives, their dreams—or the latest Martha escapade.

When September arrived, with it came one of the most difficult adjustments Virginia had faced in her entire life. Mindy was off to the local schoolhouse to begin her days as a student. She looked so small. So vulnerable. So sweet. It made Virginia weep. This was her little girl. The shy one. The one who clung to her. And now she was going off to face the world. Alone. Well, not exactly alone. Jonathan and Virginia both walked with her on her first day, and one or the other continued to do so for the remainder of the first week. Then Mindy announced in quite grown-up fashion that she knew the way down the country road. She could walk the mile on her own, she explained, and would meet up with the Ellison kids from the next farm over. That brought another tear to Virginia's eye.

Every afternoon when she thought it time for Mindy to return, Martha pushed a straight-backed chair over to the kitchen window. She climbed up on her perch to be the first to announce her big sister's appearance. Though she enjoyed the extra attention she received being the only child in the house for some period of each day, she loved Mindy and missed her during those hours of school.

The change of seasons into autumn was so subtle it hardly was noticed. Still Damaris and Slate stayed on. There were frequent letters posted to and received from the West, and occasional phone calls made from town. But nothing was said to Virginia until one day when the two women were working a flower bed together, tucking plants in for the coming winter.

"You must think I'm planning to stay forever," Damaris began.

Virginia looked up from the rose she was trimming back.

"It's been wonderful having you," she said simply.

Damaris continued to heap mulch around the roots of the bush Virginia was trimming. "I've had some thorough talks with your uncle Luke. He says that Mother's heart is continuing to weaken. I find it hard to go home thinking that something . . ." She didn't complete the thought.

Virginia went suddenly still, her heart constricting. "Did he say . . . when?"

Damaris eased back from her kneeling position and

shook her head. "He doesn't know. Not really. Anytime. But who can say? Sometimes even the weakest heart can go on beating for a long time. But if it doesn't upset your household too much, I'd like to stay for another week or so. I'd like to be here if anything . . ." Once again, she did not finish her statement.

"Of course," said Virginia, swallowing away the lump in her throat.

"Thank you." Then Damaris's voice picked up on a cheerier note. "Did you know that Slate wants to stay on?"

"Jonathan told me."

"They get along well together, don't they? Both with their love of horses and all."

"Like two peas," responded Virginia with a chuckle.

"He does seem to be a help to Jonathan."

"A big help to me too," Virginia was quick to say. "Jonathan never would have found the time to finish the trim and paint the rooms without him. Slate now works with the horses almost as much as Jonathan does."

"He sure does love the animals."

"He's a good boy," said Virginia, her eyes misting as she thought back to the incident in the corral with small Martha. Slate was now handling the stallion Warrior with the same sure hand as Jonathan. But Warrior had been moved to a new corral much farther away from the house. Jonathan did not want to take any chances. As an added precaution he had nailed chicken wire all along the bottom of the nearest corral fence. Flying hooves and tiny tots did not go well together.

"Yes," she added, "I hope his folks will agree to him remaining here with us."

Jonathan brought the letter home with him. They knew by the return address that it would indicate if Slate had permission to stay as requested or was to accompany his grandmother home at the end of the month.

Virginia thought the boy would tear the letter open then and there and inform all of them of the decision. But Slate accepted the letter from Jonathan's outstretched hand and went wordlessly from the house. She heard the door click shut behind him and saw him cross the yard, the letter still in his hand.

He headed straight for the barn. Virginia assumed he was going to the loft to read the letter in private. It was not until that moment she realized just how important the news would be to the boy. If he was instructed to return home, he would do so, but he would be deeply disappointed. He loved the work with the horses.

"O Lord," Virginia began without conscious thought—then checked herself. She would not tell the Lord what to do. He knew best. "Thy will be done," finished Virginia meekly. She turned back from the window.

Not many minutes had passed when they heard a wild whoop. Slate was running back across the yard, the letter waving over his head. With each leap in the air, another shout rang out. It appeared that Jonathan had himself a co-worker.

They had a bit of warning. Not much, but enough for all to gather around her bed and give her one final embrace and whispered words of love. And then it was over. So quickly. So peacefully. Grandmother Withers had slipped away from them to a home far better than any Virginia could offer her.

Family and friends gathered in their little church to

celebrate her homegoing. The day was decked with sun-shine, the slight breeze causing autumn-colored leaves to drift gently onto the graves of those who already had taken the journey before her.

Virginia's eyes were dry as she stood in the close clus-ter of family. She had wept. She would weep again. But for the moment she had no tears. Her heart was numb, her mind wrung dry of ability to think or feel.

People around her moved and spoke and touched her arm with comforting hands, but she was far away, trying to work through what it would be like to have a living room without an invalid's bed. A morning without a cheery greeting. A supper hour without a thankful nod and smile. Afternoon teatime without shared chats.

The children will miss you so much came to her clearly as she turned from the grave.

And then she wept.

———

Damaris packed her bags and caught the train as she had planned. Virginia was truly sorry to see her go. And now she would travel alone, with young Slate staying to help Jonathan. Virginia was undecided who was the most pleased by the arrangement—Jonathan, who desperately needed the help; she herself, who would enjoy seeing more of her husband; or Slate, who adored the horses.

The household adjusted itself to the new living ar-rangements. Grandmother's things were removed from the living room. The extra space looked bare and empty, and Virginia turned away from the sight of it with a pang in her heart. Slate took the guest room upstairs. With the nights cooler now, it was much better for him to share the house than use the barn loft.

A blanket of loneliness seemed to have settled over

Virginia's world. She had known she would miss Grandmother Withers, but she had not realized what a deep sense of loss she would feel. Though she could not—would not—wish Grandmother Withers back, she felt her days had somehow lost a good deal of meaning. Each new bit of learning that Mindy brought joyfully home from school, each new word that Martha added to her vocabulary, each new recipe or pattern found and tried—all reminded Virginia that she now had no one to share the little details of life with, moment by moment, as she had with Grandmother Withers.

There were many days she went about her tasks with a heavy heart, blinking back tears. There were many nights when she buried her head in her pillow, hoping her weeping would not disturb Jonathan's sleep.

When winter's chill moved in around them, wrapping them in snow-white blankets, with swirling icy fingers to pinch cheeks and chins, Virginia knew it would be a very long time until spring returned.

———

With the arrival of Christmas, Virginia and Jonathan carried on for the sake of the children, doing the same things they had done since they had started their lives together. But it wasn't the same. Virginia kept remembering past Christmases, with Grandmother Withers.

On the thirty-first day of December they celebrated Martha's second birthday. The excitement in her face shone in the glow of the candles, and she ate birthday cake until Virginia feared she'd be sick. But even though Virginia was able to smile and offer all the right responses, her heart still cried, *Wouldn't Grandmother have enjoyed this?*

January's cold intensified, and Jonathan took Mindy to school each day in the cutter and picked her up again at day's end. In between, the two menfolk tried to keep the stock fed and the barns cleaned. Virginia spent her days saying, "no, no," to a lively Martha and trying to keep the fires going while she did her household chores.

When February arrived with a break in the weather, Virginia felt a need to break free of her gloom. She asked Jonathan about the possibility of a visit with her grandmother. An older, wiser person—someone like Grandmother Withers—was what her heart was yearning for. Jonathan seemed to understand her need and nodded in agreement. "I'll take you over there and go on into town. Pick you up on my way back."

Virginia bundled Martha up and carried her to the car. She wished she could have time with Grandma Marty alone, but she knew Slate would not be able to watch Martha and get much of anything done in the barn.

When Virginia climbed from the car and reached for the child, Jonathan stopped her. "She can ride along with me. Let you have this time without chasing after her."

Virginia smiled her thanks and pointed out the bag with Martha's things for the day. He grinned and waved her on with, "We'll manage just fine, won't we, Martha?"

Virginia was warmly welcomed with a long embrace and ushered into a kitchen smelling of spices and hot cider.

"I was just telling Pa we ought to run on over and see how you're doin'. But he hates the icy roads more each year. So here we sat—just thinkin' of ya an' prayin' for ya but still wonderin' about ya."

Virginia removed her heavy coat and took her time hanging it on a peg. She couldn't speak. Not yet.

"Pa's out in the barn. Should I call—"

But Virginia stopped her with a hand on her arm. "Not yet, Grandma. I need to talk with you first."

Later over hot cider she began pouring out her heart.

Her feeling of loss. Her loneliness for the woman she had grown to love. Her concern that she might not get over it. Her difficulty in explaining it to Jonathan, who watched her with concern in his eyes. She knew he wanted to help, but didn't know quite how.

Grandma Marty understood. She did not even have to say so. Virginia could see it in her eyes.

"It takes time. Time and God," she told Virginia. "I was told that years ago when I lost someone. At the time, it wasn't a'tall what I wanted to hear. But it happened— just that way. Oh, not that ya ever forget. Not ever. But life has a way of movin' on. New things happen. New people come into our lives. God does not leave us stalled forever. He just nudges us forward. Pushes us on out. Urges us to look for new meanin' in life. An' it's there. It's always there. Somethin' new to live for. Somethin' to give life its zest again."

Virginia listened carefully, sniffling and wiping tears.

"An' it might happen even sooner than ya think. When least expected. You'll wake up one mornin' an' the sun will be a little brighter. The sky a little bluer. Your heart a little lighter. And you'll feel God. Comfortin'. Sort of like . . . smilin' on ya. Then you'll know. You'll know right then that healin' is on the way. That yer gonna make it. The darkest days are finally over."

She patted Virginia's hand, her own smile a little wobbly. She wiped her eyes with the lace-trimmed hankie tucked in her sleeve.

"The most beautiful part is, when ya do get to the other side of grief, ya suddenly realize that you're stronger. You've learned and grown. You know how to hang on tighter. To lean on Him who holds us. That's the beautiful part. But ya don't see that right away. You have to stand back and look at it from a distance like."

It was so good to just sit and listen to someone who

understood her feelings, her thoughts, her desires. It gave her courage. She just had to hang on and let God do the rest. In time, He would bring about the renewing and healing of the heart she needed. In time. Virginia would lean on Him. And wait.

———

March and April meant that each day was a little warmer. A little longer. Buds began to swell on the tree limbs, and shrubs opened up new blossoms. A tulip bloomed. Another, joined by a hyacinth. A robin chose early mornings to perch in the cherry tree and sing as if its heart was overflowing. Martha begged to play out-doors, and the faithful Murphy greeted her with sloppy kisses. Virginia couldn't help but laugh one afternoon as she watched the two of them standing as close as possible to a puddle without actually being in it. "Now, Mu'ph, you can't go in there," she admonished with a chubby finger in his face. The washing machine would be doing double duty this spring.

Virginia stood on the porch one morning, breathing in great draughts of fresh spring air. She thought of seeds and gardens and rows of fresh green vegetables and breeze-tossed flowers. She watched Martha pick up the dog dish and try to urge a reluctant Murphy to clean up his plate. She smiled. Her heart felt lighter. Almost whole again. And then it hit her—she was moving beyond her grief to joy again. Grandma Marty was right. God was right there. Beside her. No, even closer than that. Within her.

———

A month later Virginia moved into Jonathan's arms

after they had retired, and pressed her cheek up against his.

"I have a bit of news you might be interested in," she whispered.

She felt his arms tighten. "And that would be?"

She smiled in the darkness. Eager to tell him, yet savoring the moment. "Can you guess?" she teased.

"Tell me," he said.

"You are going to be a father again."

She had more that she was going to say, but she couldn't. Not just now. Not until Jonathan relaxed his embrace so she could catch her breath again.